Python!

DISCARD

by

Brian Moses

BRIAN MOSES is one of Britain's favourite children's poets but PYTHON is his first novel.

Brian also visits schools to run writing workshops and perform his own poetry. To date he has visited well over 2500 schools and libraries throughout the UK. He has made several appearances at the Edinburgh Festival and has taken his poetry and percussions shows to International schools in Germany, Belgium, France, Switzerland, Spain, Iceland and Ireland. At the request of Prince Charles he spoke at the Prince's Summer School for Teachers in 2007 at Cambridge University.

Two of Brian's poetry books are also published by Caboodle - *The Budgie Likes to Boogie* and *The Great Galactic Ghoul*.

The Budgie Likes to Boogie is also available as a kindle download from the Amazon kindle store at the special price of £1.71

Brian is represented by Authors Abroad who can be contacted at www.authorsabroad.com or tel: 01535 656015

Brian's websites are www.brianmoses.co.uk,
www.poetryarchive.org/brianmoses
and www.authorsabroad.com/brianmoses

Brian's blog for children and teachers is
brian-moses.blogspot.com

Follow Brian on twitter @moses_brian

Chapter One

The snake had lived in the loft for as long as Daniel could remember. He was eleven now, and he supposed that he must have been four or five when his father had brought it home. That was the only time he'd really seen it - no more than three feet long and no thicker than his wrist. He remembered seeing it in a cardboard box. His dad had opened up the flaps till it was just wide enough for him to take a look. His mother wouldn't even peep. "If that thing stays, then I go," she'd shouted. His dad had smiled, "It'll live in the loft," he'd said, "You won't even know it's there."

Other kids had fathers who were office workers or lorry drivers or shopkeepers, but Daniel's dad was different, he handled snakes at Barhampton Zoo. He'd done it for years. There was nothing he didn't know about snakes. He loved to perform to a crowd of visitors, to hear them gasp and watch them shudder.

Daniel knew the routine. His dad would ask for complete quiet. Then he'd tell the crowd that he'd been bitten so many times that the next one could be fatal." The antidote won't work on me now," he'd tell them, "I've had so much of the stuff that the next bite might be the last." But it wasn't, somehow he'd pull through.

There'd be regular hospital trips. It was as if Daniel were acting in a video that he'd seen too many times already. He knew exactly what was going to happen. He'd walk with his mum through the front doors of the hospital to be greeted by the receptionist. She would say something about the weather and joke that she didn't need to tell them which way to go. Then they'd find his Dad, propped up on pillows, a huge bandage round his arm where he'd been bitten once again. He remembered the last visit. What a way to start a new year! The second day of 1980.

"I was stupid," Daniel's dad had said to his mum. "I was careless, I took a chance."

His mum's voice had been icy. She'd had enough, he could tell. "I can't take much more of this Peter, I'm living on a knife edge, it isn't fair on me or Daniel. I'm not asking you to leave the zoo, but you must do something safer. My nerves won't take much more."

Daniel knew it was serious. She only called his dad Peter when she was really upset. At all other times it was Pete. Just then one of the nurses had called to take his dad's temperature. She'd turned to his mum, "I should think he'll be home tomorrow," she'd said, "There don't appear to be any complications and the swelling is going down."

Daniel's mum had given her a weak smile. "And we don't want him back again," the nurse had continued.

After she'd gone Daniel had listened to the hospital radio on his dad's headphones. He'd caught snatches of what his mum and dad were saying to each other.........can't take it anymore............ten years too long........horrible nightmares............ask for a transfer to a different part of the zoo....

That had been his mum speaking. Daniel had switched off the radio and paid attention. His Mum had lowered her voice but he'd still caught what she was saying. "If I can't force you to stop handling the things Peter then I will insist that you get rid of that creature in our loft." Peter again, she was obviously worked up.

"Either it goes, or I go, and I'm serious this time,"

But the snake had remained and it was Daniel's Mum who was true to her word. She didn't move far, just across town to stay at Daniel's grandma's. Daniel had tried living there too at first but it wasn't ideal. His grandma's house was small and he'd had to sleep downstairs on the settee. He didn't mind at first as it got him away from the snake. But it was a longer journey to school involving two buses and Daniel was late on a number of occasions.

His Mum and Dad were still talking to each other and as the weeks went on it was decided that Daniel should live at his dad's house in the week and go to his mum's at weekends and holidays. Daniel was far from happy to go back to living with a snake in the loft but he had been missing playing with his friends after school.

"I don't like the arrangement," Daniel's mum told him "but I can't take any more of living with your dad. He's so stubborn about that snake and I was going crazy in that house on my own, thinking about that awful creature."

Now if someone had asked Daniel if he was happy, he wouldn't have known how to reply. This was his life and he lived it. He was conscious, of course, that other children did different things, came from different homes, had mums who welcomed them home after school, gave them their tea. But that didn't happen to Daniel. He went home, raided the biscuit tin, watched TV and did his homework. His dad would then appear between six and seven to cook some food.

****

Each evening Daniel walked home from school with his best friend Errol Well actually 'walking' is probably the wrong word to describe Errol's movements. He had long legs and fancied himself as a future Olympic runner. Everywhere he went he seemed to be in training for something or other. Daniel ran along beside him but he struggled to keep up.

Errol lived in the next but one house where his dad wrote children's books for a living, He wrote about his childhood in the Caribbean. Errol's mum was a teacher in a local primary school. Each time they went back to Errol's house, his dad would take a break from his writing and welcome them in. Tonight was no exception.

Errol's dad beamed as he opened the door

"Come in, come in, good to see you Daniel, would you like some cake?"

"Yes please." Daniel knew that he'd be given a wedge of fruit cake or date and walnut. It was always delicious.

"Well, what have you done at school today?"

"Nothing much," Errol answered.

"We did!" Daniel spluttered through a mouthful of cake, "We started our new project on World War Two, it's going to be really good. We had to decorate our topic books and Sammy Lock drew pictures of bombers and tanks and flames everywhere and people being blown up, and Miss told him it wasn't what she wanted and made him do it again."

"What did you draw on your book Errol?" his dad asked.

"I can't remember, I'll tell you later. We're off to play now."

Errol's dad smiled, "Always in a rush you too, go on then."

Just as they were leaving Errol's dog came running in from the garden. She was a small and wiry mongrel, a bit of terrier, a bit of Jack Russell. A creature that always looked as if she was having a bad hair day. The dog's name was Sasha but Errol had nicknamed her 'Loo Brush.' "Well, she looks like one," he said once by way of explanation. "And she's always sticking her nose into unpleasant places."

Loo Brush was certainly not going to leave them alone. She tagged their heels along the street to Daniel's door. Errol said something that he always said at this point, "Let's go in and listen."

Daniel sighed. Most kids had friends round to watch TV or play games but all his friends ever wanted to do was to listen out for the snake.

They let themselves into his house. It wasn't like Errol's where an atmosphere of warmth reached out and grabbed you. Errol's house was tidy and neat, the rooms were white or yellow and it was as if Errol's parents had captured a piece of the Caribbean and trapped it inside their home. By contrast Daniel's house was always dark and it felt cold, even on warm days. To Daniel it was more than cold, it was menacing. The snake seemed to dominate his thoughts from the moment he stepped inside. Errol felt nothing of this, he was just excited by the thought of hearing the creature moving about.

They climbed the stairs to Daniel's room, opened the door and stared at the ceiling.

"You remember when that little dog got stuck in a badger's set," said Errol, "It was on the news a while ago. Well, they used a heat sensitive machine to show pictures on a screen. You could see the shapes of the badgers moving around."

Daniel shrugged his shoulders, "So what?"

"Well, I wish we had one," Errol continued, "We could shine it on your ceiling and see the snake's outline. We'd be able to watch it moving."

Daniel shivered. That was the last thing he'd want to do.

He knew the snake was up there, waiting for him, sizing him up. It knew Daniel was there in the room below. It was biding its time. One day it would come for him. One day Daniel would wake from his nightmare and instead of sheets wrapped round him, he'd discover coils of snake slowly squeezing the breath from his body.

He heard Errol again, "I'd be really excited if we had a snake in our loft.

Couldn't we look at it Daniel, can't we take a peep?"

"No way," Daniel shouted. Look, just watch my lips will you, NO WAY!"

The loft had been declared out of bounds to Daniel from the moment the snake had arrived. Not that he could have got up there anyway without someone's help. You needed to swing yourself up from a stepladder on the landing. It was a tricky thing to do and one which threatened to topple the ladder.

They listened in silence once more.

"I'd really love to hear it moving again," Errol said.

Daniel was still annoyed with Errol, "I've told you," he snapped, "it won't move around much, it spends a lot of time sleeping. Surely you've been to the zoo and seen the snakes. Even if you tap on the glass as hard as you can, they don't move. They're the most unexciting creatures I know. Look, I really don't care about snakes, can we do something else now?"

Daniel's father cared about snakes though, his face lit up when he talked about them, and he did talk about them, all the time. Daniel knew a whole bundle of facts about snakes. He knew that pythons quite often grew to 6.25 metres in length. He knew that the most venomous snake in the world had enough venom to kill a quarter of a million mice and that it lived in the sea and not on land; and he knew about the python in the loft, every fact about the creature's size, weight and habits.

Perhaps if Daniel had shown an interest in snakes then his father would have shown more of an interest in him. They could have shared the enthusiasm together, but it was hopeless. Daniel did try, but it was fear that prevented him, fear of what he might be letting himself in for if he began to think of snakes as pleasant creatures.

"I'm hungry again," Daniel said, "Let's go and see what's in the biscuit tin."

Daniel knew that Errol liked coming over to his house. He seemed to like the freedom of an empty house. Loo Brush yapped around their feet hoping for broken biscuits but everyone was out of luck this time. So they sat and watched television till the News came on and Daniel switched it off. A couple of minutes later the back door slammed and his dad walked in. He was home early. Most probably that meant that the snake needed feeding and he'd be off out again later to see what he could catch.

Daniel knew that his father had turned into a cold and ruthless killer of small creatures. If the snake was hungry then it was dangerous. So it was fed rats, mice, birds, chickens. Daniel imagined small bones like hieroglyphs, patterning the floor of the cage. His father went ratting with the doberman next door. He'd once taken Daniel along but he'd seen that the boy had hated the killings and he'd never asked him again

Daniel understood how snakes eat, how they can unhinge their jaws to take in a big meal. His dad had told him how a snake could swallow a whole deer sometimes, he'd seen pictures. He imagined the snake in the loft, lying there, a huge bulge in his neck, digesting, digesting.

"Daniel," his dad called, "We're eating early tonight."

"It's OK, "he called back, "Errol's just going."

"Call for me tomorrow," Errol said, as he slipped out the front door with Loo Brush then crouched down in a sprinting position. "Start us off, Daniel" he called, "We're just going to race to the end of the street and back."

****

"Have you seen your grandad this week?" Daniel's dad asked when he'd closed the door.

"I'll try and call in tomorrow, on my way home."

Daniel's grandad lived a few streets away. He'd lived on his own for the past three years since his wife had died. She'd always looked after him around the house and to begin with he'd been totally confused. Daniel's mum had helped get him back on his feet again but it wasn't easy. Although he'd got by for almost forty years with only one arm, the shock of his wife's death had made him almost helpless again. Daniel's dad used to tell him to "shake himself out of it" but it took a long time. "That one-arm bandit could help himself more," his dad would say, rather unkindly.

Daniel didn't mind visiting his grandad, fetching his paper and tobacco from the corner shop, but his grandad was just as potty about snakes as Daniel's dad was. You'd have thought that after losing his arm from the effects of a snake bite, he wouldn't have wanted anything more to do with them, but he did. Snakes, snakes, snakes, it was all his family talked about.

Daniel listened to his father as he held snake handling sessions at the zoo. On and on and on and on. Everyone asking the same questions. Does it bite? Is it poisonous, is it dangerous, can it kill you? Daniel's dad would tell them how you've got to respect a snake. A snake would never be your friend, he'd say, you'd got to treat it carefully, treat it with consideration. Daniel thought that his dad ought to have treated his mum with a little more consideration.

The snake must be huge now. Daniel knew that you shouldn't put any weight on the ceiling between the joists in the loft. His friend's father put his foot through the bedroom ceiling on one occasion. Daniel had been taken to see the hole. But what if the snake was curled up there, what if it grew too heavy and crashed through the ceiling into his room. He could see it hanging there in a shower of plaster and debris, tail wrapped round a pipe in the loft, a malevolent stare as it eyed him up as a possible source of food.

Later that night, lying in bed, Daniel was hoping that his dad might come upstairs and say good night to him. Occasionally he'd tell him an amusing story about the zoo and it would be almost like old times again. But most nights his dad would fall asleep in front of the television and Daniel would find himself listening out for the slightest noise from the loft. If the snake was wakeful and moving about, then Daniel would be alert, until the snake found some new place to curl up.

If it was a blustery night outside, Daniel worried that the wind had shifted the trap door. He worried that his dad had forgotten to bolt the cage and that somehow the snake was able to slither free. He would picture the black gap where the trap door had slipped. He knew that even if he were able to get hold of the steps, he still wouldn't be able to bring himself to climb them and try to close the gap. But he could hear the snake, he could hear it slithering, getting closer to the opening. And he knew what would happen then.

And if only the snake were the only thing he had to worry about. Unfortunately for Daniel there was usually something else that occupied his mind as he lay awake in the darkness. How on earth could he keep clear of Kelly Horton and her gang?

Chapter Two

Kelly was mean. She was bigger than Daniel and looked as if she was set on course for a career as a female wrestler. There weren't many boys in the seaside town of Barhampton who could stand up to her. All the usual notions of chivalry such as looking after the weaker sex and not hitting girls flew straight out the window when Kelly Horton got hold of you. She'd twist your arm, or kick your shins, or hit where it really hurt, leaving you rolling around on the floor in excruciating agony.

Kelly's mates were as bad. Dolly Spears would often hold you down while her leader did the dirty work, then she'd move in for a final slap or punch of her own.

Louise Lowe reminded Daniel of his father's python. She had wrap-around arms that stretched like elastic. Any embrace from Louise was likely to leave you gasping for breath and rubbing bruised ribs.

And then there was Selena Soames with the kind of voice that could blast you off your feet at fifty paces. Someone made up a rhyme about her once:

Better keep well clear of Selena
she makes more noise than a vacuum cleaner.

No one could quite discover what had happened to the boy who started off the rhyme. It was rumoured that the whole gang laid in wait for him one night, gave him the full works and then sent him home with his mouth full of mud.

All in all, it was wise to avoid the Horton gang at all times, and if possible, never be walking the streets by yourself. Fortunately Barhampton had a network of alleyways that could offer escape routes and hiding places if the gang were spotted coming your way. But if you were unfortunate to turn a corner and run straight into them your best defence was to yell and keep on yelling till some kind-hearted Neighbourhood Watch member came to see what all the noise was about.

At school this year, it was OK. The gang had moved on to the comprehensive school next door and couldn't get at you in school hours. The danger time was walking home. That was when safety in numbers was your best bet and Daniel usually chose to stick with Errol and Errol's friend Paul, even if it meant jogging or sprinting or whatever sort of training Errol was keen on at the time.

But tonight Daniel was alone. He was in the football team and had stayed behind for a practice session but now wished that he hadn't.

His way of getting home on his own was to wait until adults came along who were going in his direction and then to fall in behind them. He reasoned that if adults were around, then Kelly would think twice about ordering her gang to attack.

Tonight looked as if it would be all right. Daniel mooched along behind two mums with pushchairs. They lived close by and Daniel felt sure he'd be able to keep clear of Kelly if he stuck with them. Then disaster struck as they all stopped and turned in to someone's front garden. Daniel hung around for a bit, bending down and pretending to search for something in his bag, but when he looked up again the garden was empty. He was alone in the street.

On occasions like this he usually slunk along like a fox expecting to hear, at any moment, the loud baying of hounds, but this time he lost his nerve completely and ran down the next street.

He just managed to stay on his feet as he swept round the corner and almost collided with Dolly Spears and Louise Lowe. The python arms made a grab for his coat and held on to it. Daniel wriggled and squirmed, then with one almighty yank, tore himself free of the coat. He turned and headed back the way he had come straight into the path of Selena and Kelly. His jumper was twisted round in Kelly's hands while Selena wound his arms behind his back. He gazed into their grinning faces and felt sheer terror, the kind of terror that a small fish must feel when about to be devoured by a bunch of hungry piranhas.

"We are lucky girls," crooned Kelly, "Our little fly trap has caught us a fly. And what a tasty meal he is too."

Daniel wanted to spit in her face, but he knew he couldn't afford to wind her up anymore so he looked away.

"We spent a long time planning the perfect ambush," Kelly went on, "And now you've shown us how well we've succeeded."

Daniel tried to speak but his voice was croaky, "What do you want?"

"Tell him Louise," Kelly said.

"What we want," hissed Louise, "is you. Just look on us as scientists who need a subject for their experiment."

Daniel was really worried. He'd expected a succession of kicks and punches and as yet nothing had happened. But they'd got something planned for him and he felt certain that he wouldn't enjoy it.

He felt claws grip his arms even tighter as the gang moved along the street. He opened his mouth to yell but Dolly covered it with her hand. He tried to scream but nothing sounded.

At the end of the street was an overgrown yard that

contained a number of car wrecks among the tangled weeds and the rubbish that was thrown in there. Kelly let go of his jumper and he briefly thought of breaking free, but the others tightened their grips. Kelly kicked against the yard gate and it opened a little, giving just enough space to allow the gang to slip through taking Daniel with them. Once inside, with the gate pushed shut, Kelly turned to Daniel.

"You're a lucky lad," she said, "You are the first boy to be invited to take part in our gang's little experiment. It's a great honour and one that I'm sure you will remember for the rest of your life".

He heard sniggers from the other three. What on earth did they have planned? Whatever it was he felt sure that it would be painful and he just hoped he wouldn't cry.

"Usually," said Kelly, "We'd give you a walloping and send you on your way, but lately we've grown tired of doing that. You could say that we've grown up a bit and now we want to try something different."

Horrific visions filled Daniel's head. Would they throw him into the canal to see if he could swim? He couldn't, he'd sink. Would they cut his hair off and felt tip his head with a message that wouldn't scrub off? Would they tie him up somewhere and keep him there like a huge pet rabbit? Whatever it was he wished they'd let him know so that he could begin to think how he might escape.

Kelly moved closer. "You, my friend, are going to be kissed. You are going to be snogged by the best snoggers in town. And we want to see just how well you can snog too. Won't that be delightful?"

Daniel was absolutely horrified. He'd been prepared for anything that the gang's crazy minds could dream up but not this. The thought of Kelly's lips on his made him shudder. He felt weak in the knees. If the others hadn't been holding him up he thought that he would have collapsed.

"My go first," Kelly smiled, but it wasn't a smile. Daniel saw himself looking into the face of Medusa and wished that he were stone.

She puckered her lips and inched closer. He turned his head away but felt hands push it back. He screwed up his lips and raised his head. Again hands forced him down. But no way would he let this hideous event take place. He tried to wrench himself free of the vice like grip and felt fingers pinching his rib cage. He yelled and at that moment Kelly kissed him.

It was no brief kiss. She had limpet lips that suctioned on and wouldn't let go. No matter how hard he squirmed and wriggled and fought, the torment went on. He pretended to give up and the hold on him weakened. "I want to kiss him now," he heard Louise say. "You've had all the fun so far."

It was a nightmare, wasn't it? Surely he'd wake soon and discover that this whole horrific episode had simply been a trick of his subconscious imagination? Then Louise took a step closer and somewhere Daniel found a reserve of strength that he didn't know he had.

Like some Greek hero breaking free of the chains that bound him to a rock, Daniel shook off the hands that pinned him down. With one huge leap he scrambled onto the roof of one of the old wrecks and then jumped across bonnets and roofs till he reached the top of the wall which surrounded the yard.

Behind him he heard shrieks of laughter and he risked one swift look before plunging from the wall to the pavement below. He'd left his coat and his bag with his football boots in the yard, but it didn't matter. He was rid of them and he didn't stop running till he made it back home. Fortunately his front door key had been in his jeans pocket and not in his coat. Gratefully he opened the door and stepped inside. He slammed the door behind him and sank down onto the floor.

****

It was some time before Daniel felt calm enough to pick up the phone and dial Errol's number. His dad answered first, Errol was eating a sandwich while watching TV.

"Hi, I was going to call you later," Errol said. "Kelly's gang were on the prowl, you didn't meet up with them did you?"

"Too right," Daniel replied, "I met them. Listen, can you come round, I need to talk to you."

"Sure, just give me a couple of minutes to finish my sandwich and then I'll be there."

When Daniel opened the door to his friend, it was obvious to Errol that something awful had taken place. "You look terrible," he said, really shocked. So what did they do to you? Are you hurt?"

Daniel felt embarrassed. He couldn't decide how much to tell Errol. "They mugged me," he said.

"Where are you hurt?" Errol asked again, "Have you got bruises?"

Daniel sat on the stairs and told Errol what had happened. Errol whistled. "Wow!" he said, "That sort of thing can scar you for life!" Then he laughed. Daniel looked upset.

"Sorry," said Errol, "I shouldn't have laughed. it must have been terrible. Do you think they'll try it again?"

"You bet your life they will. This is not just kiss chase, it's kiss torture. I think I might just crack up if I have to go through that again." Daniel shivered. "The problem now is how do we fight back, how can we stop them?"

"Well my mum won't kiss my dad when he's been eating garlic," said Errol.

"Garlic!" Daniel shouted. "I can't stand garlic."

"Well which do you like the least," Errol asked, "Eating garlic or being slobbered over by Kelly Horton?"

"There's no choice," Daniel muttered, "Where do we buy garlic?"

"Don't forget there's another benefit from eating garlic," said Errol, "Vampires will leave you alone."

At that moment, Daniel thought that even meeting up with a vampire would be more bearable, compared to the sort of treatment he'd received that afternoon from Kelly and her gang. He even began to think that if he were making a list of his greatest fears, the snake in the loft might not have scored top marks that evening.

****

The next morning Daniel found his coat and bag on his doorstep, with a message that read - "We'll be looking out for you." This was followed by several kisses. Daniel screwed up the note and flung it away. He set off for school with Errol and he had to admit that sometimes even Errol got on his nerves. He was running and jumping round Daniel while at the same time teasing him about what had happened with Kelly Horton.

"Bet I know what nightmare you had last night Daniel. I bet she was dreaming about you too. Whatever you do, don't walk home alone tonight, she might grab you for another slobber."

"Errol, just leave it will you. And if you mention it to anyone else I'll never forgive you."

As it happened Errol didn't need to say anything. Kelly's gang must have been really active the previous night because two other boys in Daniel's year had been kiss tortured. Various bits of advice were being offered as to what might be done in that situation but those who had suffered just shook their heads and said how impossible it had been to do anything.

"I kept my mouth closed for as long as I could" one of them said, but that Louise pinched my nose. I held my breath until I absolutely had to move my lips apart and then she pounced."

Daniel shivered, remembering what he'd gone through. Everyone else shivered too, imagining what their friends had gone through.

You put up with being kissed by your Great Aunt Lucy at Christmas, particularly if she presses a five pound note into your hand at the same time, and you put up with being kissed by your mum as you leave for school in the morning. But how on earth could you cope with being a target for the massed lips of the Horton gang?

At lunchtime they discussed possible solutions to their problem although most of these were rejected almost immediately. No one had much enthusiasm for anything and even football had been abandoned.

"It's Ok during term time," said Errol's friend Paul, "But what happens in the holidays? We can't always avoid being on our own then. We'll all be at risk."

Paul was worried. There was only a week or so before the start of the Easter holidays. His parents were out at work most of the time and he was left on his own. "I won't be able to go out," he said, "I'll be a prisoner in my own home."

Daniel understood what he meant. He'd have the same problem.

****

That afternoon Mr. Metcalfe, Daniel's teacher, wondered

what was up with the boys in his class. Usually they played about, shouted out, acted the fool, but this afternoon they lacked their usual spark. They seemed troubled, preoccupied. Still, it made for a quiet afternoon and Mr. Metcalfe was all in favour of that.

By home time he had an idea that Kelly Horton and her gang were planning something. You don't spend twelve years in the classroom without learning to pick up on snatches of conversation and Mr. Metcalfe had developed extremely sensitive hearing.

He'd had a lot of trouble with the Horton gang the previous year. He'd talked to their parents but their attitude seemed to be, "Well life is tough - let the kids sort themselves out." Most of the boys had stopped complaining by now. It did no good.

Kelly's dad was a fearsome character who slobbed around the house in a string vest and took occasional trips to the betting shop. Anyone who had dared to call and complain about his daughter had met with threats and abuse. The boys were terrified of the Horton gang and yet to complain would have made them seem wimps. Instead they dreamed of developing muscles overnight, turning themselves into the heroes of big action movies.

When the bell rang for end of school, anyone watching would have thought that the boys in Mr. Metcalfe's class were reluctant to leave. They delayed putting on their coats, then found excuses to nip back into the classroom, never alone, always in groups.

"Have none of you lot got homes to go to?" their caretaker called out, moving the floor polisher towards them in a threatening manner.

Finally, in a large huddle, the boys crossed the playground and paused by the school gates, before moving out into the street. Kelly and her gang could be anywhere but at least there was safety in numbers.

After a while, Daniel, Errol and Paul left the larger group and headed off towards their own street. As they drew near the gasworks they heard loud clangs. It sounded as if stones were being thrown against the huge gasometers inside the works. The boys had done this too at various times. They liked to hear the noise that stones made as they clanged against metal and the shouts of gasworks officials behind the high wall that hid them from view. All three boys peered round the next corner and saw that Kelly's gang were responsible for all the noise.

"What do we do now?" Daniel asked.

"What we do," said Errol as he started to sprint away, "is to find another route home."

Chapter Three

Mr. Metcalfe was reading.

It was just after lunch and 6M, Daniel's class, were quiet for once.

Mr. Metcalfe was a good reader. He drew you into the story, made you feel part of what was happening. He used different voices so you knew at once who was speaking.

This time the book was about two children living on their own in wartime London. It linked in with their topic work and it was a good story. Mr. Metcalfe's deep voice wove a spell around the words. All of 6M were tuned into their teacher. All, that is, except Daniel.

Daniel was finding it hard to concentrate. It happened now and again. Sometimes he'd find himself cat-napping, trying to catch up on sleep that he'd missed when he lay awake and worried about the snake. Sometimes he'd find himself wandering around the room for no real reason. Mr. Metcalfe said that he suffered from "Can't-stay-in-his-own-seat-itis", but on this occasion he was looking out the window. He kept returning to the daydream that had been bothering him ever since Mr. Metcalfe had told 6M about the German plane that had crashed-landed in their school grounds.

Daniel could see it now, a spiral of smoke falling to earth, a flash of light, a huge explosion as it hit, then flames consuming the plane. He would have cheered if he had been there. It had been a Messerschmitt R.E. 109, another victory for the RAF.

Daniel knew about planes. His collection of model

aircraft hung from his bedroom ceiling and most of the books in his bookcase were about aircraft identification. But what happened to the pilot of the plane? Did the pilot burn too, or did he come down nearby? What happened to him?

6M sniggered. Daniel had spoken aloud. Mr. Metcalfe stopped reading and stared at his class. He could be really sarcastic at times, especially towards Daniel, but at other times he helped him, perhaps more so than anyone else in the class. What would he do now?

"Daniel, would you tell us where we've got to in the story please?"

Daniel didn't know. He knew Mr. Metcalfe knew he didn't know. Would anyone help him? He looked around hopefully. Paul was grinning at him. Errol had found a tiny spider on his desk and was busy building it an obstacle course with pens and a rubber.

"Well, Daniel?"

"I don't know." Honesty always pays, his mum said, but Daniel had learnt that a swift prayer and a sorrowful look on his face were both necessary as well with Mr. Metcalfe.

"Who can tell Daniel where we are in the book?"

Several hands shot up. Daniel held his breath. Errol knew of course. He rattled it off like an express train at speed till Mr. Metcalfe was forced to apply the brakes himself. He turned back to Daniel whose breath had just escaped with a loud noise, "Why couldn't you tell me all that, Daniel?"

"I was thinking of something else."

Mr. Metcalfe looked at his class, he couldn't pass by the opportunity for a laugh or two. "What were you thinking about Daniel, whether you'll have fish fingers for tea, or were you thinking about all the work you haven't done for me today?"

6M laughed. Daniel reddened. "I was thinking about that plane, the one that crashed out there." He waved his arm in the direction of the window.

"Go on."

"Well, I was wondering what happened to the pilot, you never told us."

Well it was a long tine ago Daniel, September 1940, I believe, at the height of the Battle of Britain. It's 1980 now of course, so can anyone tell me how long ago it was?"

Several hands were raised along with one or two shouts of '40 years.'

"Well, I'm glad that some of you are on the ball with maths. And before you start asking if I was there at the time, I wasn't. I'm not that old. I wasn't born till well after the war had finished."

"How old are you?" someone called out.

"I'm not going into that at the moment," Mr Metcalfe replied.

"All I know about the pilot is that he managed to free himself from the wreckage but he was very badly burnt. He may have died from his injuries."

A freckled lad called Steven, who wore glasses and spoke very loudly called out, "My dad says that the old aerodrome they used in the war is haunted. He says that there are ghosts of all the pilots who crashed there."

Before Mr. Metcalfe could reply, Errol, who had lost his spider, leaned over and nudged Steven, "Your dad's daft. Who do you think is going to believe that?"

6M had started talking among themselves and Mr. Metcalfe shouted for silence. "Whether you believe Steven's dad's story is up to you, now I think that it is time we got on with some work."

Daniel smiled. That hadn't been much of a telling off.

Then he felt a hand on his shoulder and looked up to find his teacher by his side. He hadn't escaped after all, there was to be some kind of punishment. "I wouldn't worry too much about that pilot Daniel," Mr Metcalfe said in a gentle voice, "It was a very long time ago." Then he smiled and moved away.

6M were busy that afternoon looking up information about the war that would help them complete a number of tasks that Mr. Metcalfe had set them. Daniel worked hard for once too. He became so involved with what he was trying to find out that he forgot his problems. Towards the end of the afternoon someone asked Mr. Metcalfe a question about air raid shelters.

"You do realise, of course, that there is a huge system of tunnels under Barhampton that acted as an air raid shelter for the entire population of the town?"

Daniel knew that. One of the old tunnel entrances was in the recreation ground alongside his garden. The tunnels were cut into the chalk and you could walk from one part of the town to another over sixty feet below the surface. Everyone sheltered there to escape the bombing and lots of families made their homes down there when they were being bombed each night.

Most of the class had been down there too. Even though the entrances had been blocked off after the war it was still quite easy to find ways into the system. Kids called them the wind tunnels and all kinds of stories were told about them. There was talk of ghost trains (a miniature railway once ran through the main tunnel) and of fireballs that blew through the blackness. It was certainly spooky down there and you needed a really powerful torch to cut through the gloom.

There were newspaper reports of children getting lost in the tunnels. Anxious parents would ring the fire brigade and the firemen would search around down there for an hour or two, but usually by then the kids had found another way out.

****

The end of the day came round and again the boys were in no hurry to leave the school. Finally the school caretaker shooed them out of the cloakroom and reluctantly they crossed the playground to the street.

Kelly's gang were huddled on the corner and immediately Selena's foghorn boomed out, "Whose turn is it tonight?"

"This way," Errol said, and they started to run in the opposite direction. Several boys left the main group relying on the fact that Kelly's gang couldn't follow everyone. Errol, Paul and Daniel slid into an alleyway and had just reached the end when they realised that the Horton gang were still on their trail. They fountained out and collided with a couple of big lads from the comprehensive school. One of them landed a kick on Daniel's shin which made him wince with pain but he recovered and chased after the others.

He looked back to see the same lads being skittled again by the combined force of the Horton gang as they left the alleyway. Everyone seemed to go down on the pavement and while they were sorting themselves out, Daniel and his friends turned a corner, overtook a couple of mums with young children and then slowed to take advantage of the slight protection they offered.

They didn't look back but they did hear Selena trumpeting once more, "Don't be shy, we just want to be friendly."

"I'd rather make friends with a shoal of sharks ," Paul called back.

The mums were beginning to realise that they were in the middle of something that might turn nasty and they quickly crossed over the road. Daniel, Errol and Paul crossed too but the Horton gang stayed on the other side and flung insults across the street.

"I really don't think they're worth bothering with, what a bunch of wimps," that was Kelly's voice.

"Mummy's boys, that's all you are." Louise added, "Why don't you stand and fight?"

Fighting was one thing but risking what the Snogger Squad was now serving up was something else entirely. No self-respecting lad could ever be blamed for preferring flight to an encounter with the puckered lips of the Horton gang.

"Listen," said Daniel, my grandad lives down here. I think we should call on him and lie low for a bit. Hopefully they'll get fed up and go home."

Another fifty metres brought them to the front door of the terraced house where Daniel's grandad lived. Daniel rang the bell while the Horton gang watched from the other side of the street. "Don't think you can escape like that, we'll be waiting for you, you can't stay in there forever."

Daniel's grandad took some time opening the door but as soon as he saw the boys he stood back to let them in. "Thanks grandad, you've saved our lives."

"From those lassies across the street? You can't be serious. In my day it was the boys who chased the girls. I had angry dads knocking on my parents' door many times. They said I chased their daughters. I did too! Still don't know what I'd have done if I'd caught one!"

"You don't know these girls," said Errol, "they're fiends, harpies, witches. Anyone who falls into their clutches is dead meat."

Daniel's grandad laughed. "Now what about something to drink? I always keep a bottle of lemonade for when my grandson calls. Not that he calls very often these days, do you Daniel?"

"Sorry grandad, I'll try harder."

"Oh, I understand. It's not much for a young lad like you. I was the same at your age, although I used to have to dress up in my Sunday best when I went visiting."

Daniel's grandad moved about in his kitchen, carefully pouring the lemonade into glasses with his one arm, while the boys sat round the table and discussed tactics. If the gang were still there when they left, there was always the back entrance. They could try that.

Outside the kitchen window the sky was darkening. "It looks like you won't have to worry about those lassies, it's going to pour down soon. That'll send them scuttling off home."

Just as Daniel's grandad finished speaking there was a clap of thunder and the sound of heavy rain against the window. Daniel ran into his grandad's front room and looked out. He could see the Horton gang running down the street. It looked like they'd be OK.

When he returned to the kitchen Daniel found his grandad talking with Paul and Errol. Paul was explaining how their class at school were looking at life in World War Two. Daniel took a good look at his grandad. He must have been involved in the war in some way. He'd have been young enough to fight but with only one arm he wouldn't have been much use in the forces. He didn't speak much about the war, not like some old folk.

His mum's father was always going on about the war, where he served, what he did. He used to tell Daniel the same old stories about fighting the Germans in North Africa. Daniel smiled as he remembered the one about the scorpion that grandad found in his boot one morning, and the other occasion where he'd ate his Christmas dinner off the bonnet of a lorry in Austria. His dad's dad told plenty of stories but they were mostly about when he was a boy, the games he'd played and the fun he'd had with his mates.

Daniel listened in to what Errol was saying. He was explaining about the German plane that crashed in the grounds of the school. "Do you know what happened to the pilot?" he asked Daniel's grandad.

Daniel thought that his grandad looked rather startled by this question. He seemed reluctant to answer and when he finally spoke he appeared to be staring intently into each boy's face. "I believe he died," he said.

"Look, it was a long time ago. I put it all behind me. Lots of folk lost lots of loved ones in that war and it's not something that I care to dwell upon.

Let's leave it, all right?"

Daniel felt convinced that his grandad was hiding something. "I don't know why they make young folk rake over the past. Let sleeping dogs lie, that's what I say and I wish other folk would do the same."

"What were the tunnels like?" Paul asked.

"Well, there's something I don't mind talking about," said Daniel's grandad. "There were about three miles of them hollowed out of the chalk like a massive rabbit warren beneath Barhampton. There were twenty or so entrances up top and when the siren went to tell us that bombs would shortly be dropping, we had to stop what we were doing and hurry to the nearest tunnel entrance.

Lots of families used to sleep down there at night. They'd curtain themselves off so they had a bit of privacy and they'd cook meals on primus stoves. Some folk were so scared of going up top that they moved down there completely. They'd take the cat and the budgie down and make it a home from home."

"I'd like to go down again and have a proper look," said Errol, "We could mount an expedition, take really powerful torches and search around to see if we could find something to do with the war."

"I wouldn't if I were you," warned Daniel's grandad, "They're dangerous. You could easily get lost down there. The chalk falls in too and there's often flooding. Stay away."

The rain was still falling heavily and it occurred to Daniel that it might be safest if they left soon and tried to get home before Kelly and the gang took to the streets again. "Thanks grandad," he said. "We may need to call unexpectedly another day, is that all right with you?"

"Anytime Daniel. When you're my age time starts to drag and any visit is welcome. Say hello to your dad for me, remind him to call round at the weekend, if he can tear himself away from that snake of his."

Minutes later Errol, Paul and Daniel were speeding down their street. The rain had penetrated clothes and slicked down hair. Their feet were wet from the puddles they'd splashed through. They couldn't have been much wetter if they'd fallen into the sea. Their only consolation was that the Horton gang had abandoned the chase. The sharks were no longer circling.

****

That evening, Daniel's dad went out and left Daniel eating in front of the TV. There was an item about a Greek chap called Damocles who sat down to a huge banquet while over his head there hung a sword which was suspended from a single hair. Damocles couldn't enjoy the wonderful food on his plate because he was terrified that at any moment the hair might snap and the sword would skewer his scalp.

Daniel thought that he had a lot in common with Damocles, although in his case there were twin swords - the Horton gang and the python in the loft.

Daniel's dad came back home about seven, "I need your help," he said.

"Come on."

Daniel followed him out to the car. He had a ladder tied to the roof rack and a boot full of wood and glass from the DIY store. "Help me get the ladder off the roof first, then we can carry it upstairs."

Warning bells sounded in Daniel's head, surely his dad didn't think that Daniel would be going anywhere near that snake. His voice was croaky, "What are you going to do dad?"

"Well, first off I'm replacing that old step ladder of ours with something that will reach up into the loft without me having to risk my neck every time I swing myself into the roof. Then secondly I'm extending the python's cage. She's grown far too big for the one that I made when she first arrived. And Daniel, don't kick up a fuss but I'll need your help. You'll be quite safe, I promise you."

Daniel backed away, "I can't.... You know how I feel about that creature. "Don't ask me."

Daniel's dad stopped untying the ladder for a moment and looked down at his son. "Please help me tonight Daniel, I won't ask again. Just help me shift the wood and glass upstairs and then pass it to me while I'm on the ladder. That's all I ask. You needn't go into the loft, I'll do all that."

They took the ladder up and eased it into the loft space. "That'll be much better." Then the wood and the glass were taken up. There was an awful lot of it and Daniel wondered how big the cage would be, and more worryingly, how big the creature had grown. It must be enormous, he thought.

Soon Daniel's dad was persuading Daniel to stand on the ladder and pass wood through the hatch. At one stage he found that he could see into the loft. He drew back but then looked again.

The snake was still. His dad noticed him looking. "Don't you think that she's beautiful Daniel?"

Beautiful was not the word that sprang to mind as Daniel gazed at the python. He admitted that the woven pattern of gold, brown and black looked quite attractive, but he couldn't understand why his dad had allowed such a huge and potentially vicious killer to live and grow in their house. After all, he did work with snakes all day at the zoo, so why did he need one at home?

"I just need to feed her Daniel, if you don't want to watch then go back down for a while."

Daniel was just trying to find his footing again on the ladder when he glimpsed his father take a small still creature out of a bag in his pocket. He couldn't be absolutely certain but it looked like a baby guinea pig. He turned away in disgust and eased himself back down the ladder. He remembered his dad saying once how someone he knew bred guinea pigs for display at pet shows, and how the smallest and weakest were killed off. Presumably his dad bought them as snake food and although he understood that his dad was only taking advantage of someone else's callousness, he hated him for it. He hated him for keeping the snake and letting his mum go.

He sat downstairs and turned on the TV. He half watched *Coronation Street* and tried to blot out the image of the guinea pig disappearing down the snake's throat.

The hammering and sawing in the loft went on till late

into the night. Daniel took ages to get to sleep and when he did drop off, he had a series of bad dreams. When he woke, the dream that he remembered most vividly was where the snake had reared up in front of him, swaying terrifyingly, and its face was Kelly Horton's.

Chapter Four

Daniel was useless at forward rolls. No matter how hard he tried his body refused to do what he wanted it to do, and his forward rolls toppled over sideways in a tangle of arms and legs.

Mr. Metcalfe shook his head, "Never mind Daniel, you'll manage it one day."

P.E. was all right with Mr. Metcalfe. He never made his class feel bad about not being able to do something. He'd often told 6M about how awful he was at doing things when he was young and somehow that made it better. Then when someone did finally manage to do something that they'd been trying to do for weeks, he got really excited himself. He was OK as far as teachers go.

Daniel had just made a mess of his fourth attempt at a forward roll and had gone to sit on the benches. It was a warm afternoon and even with windows and doors open, the school hall was hot. He'd heard one of the dinner ladies saying that it was brewing up for a storm. He moved to sit by an open window but the air was still and there was no relief. As he sat watching Errol produce perfect forward rolls, he felt that a storm might well be a possibility.

The sky was darkening and Mr. Metcalfe asked Daniel to switch on the hall lights. There were six switches and his fingers raced along them all. As he reached his seat, the lights dimmed and went out.

"I asked you to put the lights on Daniel, not to fool around with them. Switch them back on immediately."

"But Mr. Metcalfe, I did put them on. It's not me, honest."

His teacher looked at him and then at the lights. They came back on. He turned to watch the next child in the line and the lights blanked once more.

"It must be ghosts," called out Steven. "My dad's seen one," he added as the hall was bathed in light once more before being plunged back into gloom.

Mr. Metcalfe's voice was stern, "If anyone is fiddling with those lights they'll be in trouble." Everyone held their hands in front of them and moved away from the switches. The on and off flashing continued. Outside in the distance 6M heard the first rumbling of thunder. They looked towards the windows.

The hall curtains were huge and heavy, the kind that are opened and closed by pulling on a rope. As the class watched, the curtains puffed out, filled with wind like the sails of a ship. They billowed out into the hall and then sank back again. After the third time this happened, Mr. Metcalfe was convinced that a wind had blown up in the face of the oncoming storm. Already the air felt cooler. The lights too had dimmed, gone out and remained out, obviously faulty. He explained what had happened to his class. They looked relieved.

But Daniel was anything but relieved. There had been no storm, just a few drops of rain and he found himself agreeing with Steven as to the cause of the strange happenings that his class had witnessed. Steven had almost hit the nail on the head when he mentioned ghosts. But Daniel was convinced that it wasn't ghosts, it was one ghost. And if they could see him, he'd be dressed in the uniform of a German Luftwaffe pilot.

****

37

If you have ever played the game of Chinese Whispers, then you will understand how stories get changed round as they are spread from mouth to mouth. By the next morning there wasn't much that 6M hadn't seen in the school hall during their PE lesson. Anyone listening to them would have been told that closed windows had blown open, the hall lights had flashed S.O.S. in Morse code signals, and the piano had picked out a tune by itself. Some of the boys claimed that they'd seen a whole squadron of German fighter planes sweep low across the playground and Daniel was asked to describe what he thought the German pilot might look like.

"My dad says that a Jerry plane did crash on our school grounds and that the pilot could easily be a ghost," said Steven. "He *has* seen one. He says that ghosts come back to places where they've been very sad."

"Should we tell Mr. Metcalfe?" asked Paul, "He might let us look for the ghost."

"You must be mad," Daniel said loudly, "he'd be more likely to lead us on a trip up Mount Everest."

"If we want to look for this ghost," said Errol, "then we'll have to look for it on our own,"

They picked up their bags and trooped into school.

In assembly, Daniel's class half-expected something to happen. The whole school was in the hall. Surely the time was right for some ghostly signal. Mrs. Francis, their head teacher, led the singing, her voice loud enough to frighten off any timid spectre.

Back in the classroom Daniel tried to forget about the plane and its pilot but at break time he found himself in the entrance hall where most of 6M were gathered around a photograph on the wall. There were several photographs in the entrance hall and if he'd thought about them at all, Daniel would have said that they were photos of previous head teachers. Above the hubbub of voices he heard Steven again.

"I keep telling you, his eyes move, they follow you. It's weird."

Daniel moved closer. The photo everyone was staring at was of a man in a peaked cap and some sort of uniform. As it was in black and white, with only his head and shoulders showing, he might have equally well been a naval officer or one of those porters in posh hotels. But in Steven's eyes, this was their German pilot.

"You have to stand back," Steven shouted, "you're too close, you won't see a thing. " With this he swiped out at anyone in his way and they all moved back.

"There's nothing to see," called Errol, "It's a trick."

"I can see it, they're moving," another voice claimed.

"Where? That's rubbish."

"It's true, I tell you."

Soon there were any number of witnesses to the strange event.

"OUT, O U T spells OUT,"

Everyone groaned. Mrs. Francis held the door while everyone filed past. Steven paused, "That picture, it's strange." Perhaps it was an accident that Errol kicked him hard at that moment, but he certainly lost all interest in telling Mrs. Francis what they'd discovered.

****

During the hour before lunch, a procession of children visited the toilets and found excuses to go back to their classrooms through the entrance hall where they paused in front of the photograph. Mrs. Francis, on her way to the car park, found two boys with the photograph in their hands, checking the back of the frame. On her return, two girls from 5R were acting suspiciously, standing on tiptoe and craning their necks for a glimpse of something. Mrs. Francis was puzzled.

After lunch she found four children on their knees in the entrance hall and no one would say what they were up to. Rumour had got around that if anyone told about the photograph they'd be sorted out by Year 6. So naturally everyone stayed tight-lipped.

Towards the end of the afternoon, Mrs. Francis called into 6M and asked if Mr. Metcalfe could do a job for her while she stayed with his class. She wanted a large bookcase moved and Mr. Metcalfe chose six boys to help him, ignoring the groans of "It's not fair" from several of the girls.

The bookcase was heavy and difficult to move. "We'll try it the Egyptian way," Mr. Metcalfe announced. "Barry, Tim, you go down to the sports cupboard and bring up six cricket stumps."

The two boys looked surprised at the request but knew better than to argue. While they were gone Mr. Metcalfe explained what he had in mind.

"When they built the Pyramids, the Egyptians used to move huge pieces of stone using round lengths of wood as rollers. Now if we place cricket stumps under this bookcase, we ought to be able to shift it more easily."

Five minutes passed by and Mr. Metcalfe was still waiting for his stumps. "Daniel, go down and chase up those boys please or school will be over before we get started."

Daniel chased along the corridor and round to the sports cupboard. It was empty. As he turned to go back he heard voices from the entrance hall. Barry and Tim, with the stumps in their arms, were staring hard at the photo of the German pilot.

"Surely you don't believe Steven's nonsense," said Daniel, "It's just a wind up."

"We didn't," Tim said, "but if you stand where we're standing, I don't think you'll feel so sure."

Daniel pushed up close to Tim and stared hard. He blinked, then rubbed his eyes. Tim was right, everyone was right, the pilot's eyes were moving. He stood in a different position. The eyes followed him. He turned away, then back. The eyes still held him.

"What on earth are you boys doing?" Mr. Metcalfe was angry. "I want a simple job done and you waste ten minutes of my time with your silly pranks. Now move with those stumps before I lose my temper."

The boys fled and within a few minutes the bookcase was in its new position. On their way back to class they stopped and stared. Where the bookcase had been, set into the floor, was the outline of a trapdoor.

****

Over a cup of tea in the staff room that evening, Mr. Metcalfe told Mrs. Francis about the incident with the cricket stumps. Something was happening, they agreed, but what? And what had it do with that photograph of Wing Commander Heatherington in the entrance hall?

Chapter Five

"So where does it lead to?"

Daniel and Errol had sneaked into school before school started and were staring at the place where the bookcase had been. "I'm not certain," said Daniel, "but I think it might lead down to the tunnels. I called in on grandad again last night and told him what we'd found. He said that there used to be an entrance to the tunnels from Barhampton School. They needed to get the children to safety when the air raid warning sounded."

"So if we lifted it up, we'd find steps and a direct route to the tunnels?"

"We might. But it doesn't look that easy to lift."

At that moment two boys from year 4 came along the corridor, "Hey Daniel," one of them called out, "If this school's haunted, where do you think we'd find the ghost? Do you think there'd be clues anywhere?"

Daniel started walking away, then called back over his shoulder, "There is no ghost, I made it up."

Out in the playground Errol was puzzled, "What did you go and say that for?"

"Look, let's keep what we know to ourselves OK?. If that pilot did crash here, and if his ghost is still hanging around somewhere, he's hardly likely to put in an appearance in the middle of a noisy school. He'd be frightened off straightaway. And he'll certainly be frightened off by everyone poking around into cupboards and dark corners calling out, here ghosty, nice ghosty, as if it's a lost kitten that they're looking for."

"Right, so what happens now?"

"My guess is that if this ghost pilot is anywhere, he's down in the tunnels. If we want to look for him, that's where we start."

"So we sneak into school at night, open the trapdoor, and make sure we know a few words of German like Hello, we're your friends. Alternatively of course, we meet up with this guy and he looks so hideous that we freak out completely. I'm not sure I want to go on with this."

"We may not be able to get into the tunnels from here. Grandad says that the entrance may have been blocked up. He showed me a map of the tunnels last night and I've been thinking. If we got in at the back of my house, I think I could find my way through to here and we could check it out from below."

"Look, Daniel," said Errol, "have you been listening to me? I said I'm not too sure I fancy this. I don't want to spend the rest of my days with my hair permanently stuck on end through having been frightened out of my wits."

"Well I'm going," Daniel said, "It's up to you what you do."

At that moment they heard the whistle being blown for start of school.

****

Later that morning it became obvious that the children at Barhampton school rather liked the idea of their school being haunted. It seemed that a full scale search of the school was taking place. Cupboards, spare rooms, dark corners, high shelves were all being explored. Mr. Higgins, the school caretaker chased children out of his store cupboards. Mrs. Francis disturbed two girls investigating her private toilet and Mr. Metcalfe caught two of his boys trying to pick the lock on the cupboard where costumes are kept for school plays. At lunchtime Mrs. Francis asked the rest of her staff if anyone knew what was going on.

"I'm mystified," she said. "Usually there's someone ready to spill the beans when something like this happens, but it seems like they've all taken a vow of silence. Anyone I ask is immediately struck dumb. I just don't understand."

"I think I'm beginning to piece something together Mrs. Francis," said Mr. Metcalfe. "I took a call just now, while you were in the dining hall. It was Mrs. Harcourt, mother of Philippa in year 1, and she asked me what I knew about a school ghost. Apparently there's a rumour spreading round that the school is haunted, and her daughter is terribly worried about it. She couldn't get to sleep last night."

"Did she say what form this ghost is supposed to take?"

"Yes she did," said Mr. Metcalfe, with a barely disguised chuckle. "She says it's the ghost of that German pilot who crashed in the school grounds."

"And do we know who started this rumour?"

"I'm afraid I do. I think that it was my class, and in particular Daniel Palmer. He's been worrying about the pilot since I told 6M about the incident as part of their topic work."

"And he's got the whole school believing in this ghost?"

"It does look that way, Mrs. Francis."

"This needs some careful thought Mr. Metcalfe, some very careful thought."

****

"You're a coward Daniel Palmer.""You're yellow, just like your grandad."

Kelly Horton was having a go.

44

It was Friday night and they were walking back from school. The boys had been reluctant to leave as usual. Kelly and her mates had given Daniel and Errol a rest for a couple of nights but now they were trailing them again. Between them were two mums with pushchairs. They looked like the same ones who had been caught in the crossfire earlier that week and they looked none too pleased about it.

"You're a coward, you've got a yellow streak..."

Selena joined in with a shout that must have been heard across town. "Hey, Banana Man, why don't you stick up for yourself?"

Daniel and Errol kept their heads down and the mums behind them.

"Off to see him again are you?" Louise this time. "Your grandad, coward of the county."

Daniel paused, long enough for one of the pushchairs to hit the back of his legs. Errol elbowed him on. "What are they on about?"

Daniel looked grim. He felt that something would snap inside him if he listened to them for much longer. He started to run.

"Cow.........ard, cow.........ard."

Perhaps they were right.

Errol came chugging along beside him. "What are they on about, what do they mean about your grandad?"

Daniel kept running. He was a coward, it was true. He was frightened of the snake in his loft and he was frightened of Kelly's gang, although after his last experience, he couldn't think of anyone who wouldn't be frightened. They'd struck again last night. It had been Steven this time who had been given the full works. He'd torn himself free eventually but not before he'd been embraced by python Louise and snogged by both Kelly and Dolly. Daniel shivered as he remembered what it had been like.

He turned into his street with Errol close behind. The Horton gang seemed to have lost interest and once inside Daniel's house, Errol asked again,

"What do they mean, about your grandad?"

"I don't know, but it's worrying me. I think I'm going round to see him now."

"You'd better be careful. Shall I see if I can come with you?"

"No, I'll be all right. I think I'd better see him on my own."

****

Daniel went over the back fence and into the recreation ground. His route was a roundabout one that took him away from any likely places where the Horton gang might be hanging out. He reached his grandad's house and knocked on the door.

His grandad was surprised to see him. "A second visit this week Daniel? Why have I become so popular all of a sudden? Or are you being chased again? I'd give anything to have lassies chasing after me. Most of the ladies I know only move fast when there's a cup of tea on offer."

"Anyway, sit down, have a drink, and what can I do for you? I told you everything I could about the tunnels the other day."

"It's not the tunnels grandad, it's just that......" Daniel trailed off, he didn't quite know how to put it.

"Well what, it can't be that bad."

Kelly Horton, one of those girls who were chasing me, she says you're a coward. And I don't know why she's saying that. It isn't true grandad, is it?"

46

Daniel's grandad didn't say anything. He looked at the wall above Daniel's head. He coughed, and Daniel thought he was going to say something but he stopped himself. Daniel had never thought of his grandad as being particularly old until that moment. He seemed to shrink down in his chair and the wrinkles on his face seemed to multiply. Finally he seemed to return from whatever journey he'd been taking in his head. He forced himself to look at Daniel.

"I made a bad mistake," he said, "you'd have known sooner or later. I was at school with Kelly Horton's grandad. He was a big lad, really handy with his fists. He had it in for me and I often went home with a split lip or a black eye. I tried to fight back but it was no use, I had no talent for scrapping. He's never stopped having a go at me, even now. He'll have told Kelly his own version of events, so I'll have to tell you mine."

"When I left school I got a job at the zoo. Just like your dad I was looking after the snakes. I was handling them regularly and I really got to like them. This was in the years just before the war. We all knew that there'd be a war but we just didn't know when. Then in 1939 we knew it couldn't be avoided. All sorts of plans were made to keep people safe if the Germans dropped bombs on us. The tunnels were built for one thing and then the zoo decided to follow the lead given by London Zoo. All the poisonous snakes were to be destroyed in case bombs hit the zoo and they escaped. It was reckoned there'd be enough panic without a load of snakes on the loose. But I was stupid, I'd grown really fond of a King Cobra. It was a wonderful creature with beautiful markings. I couldn't bear to see it killed."

"So what happened?" Daniel interrupted.

"I stole it Daniel. I stole a King Cobra from Barhampton

Zoo and I took it home with me. Don't ask me how I did it, I took some incredible chances. I just wanted to keep this beautiful creature alive. Everything went smoothly, I'd built it a home, I was fully prepared. But I took a short cut while moving the snake to its new home and it bit me on the arm."

"I struggled on and made the snake safe, but the shock was terrible and the pain was like nothing on earth. But I knew what to do and I'd come prepared. I did everything by the book, gave myself the right antidote but I was out of my head for days. I lived on my own at that time and nobody came near. I managed to crawl to the sink and drink tap water but I ate nothing for six days, just lay on the floor thinking I was going to die."

"Why didn't you crawl out the house,"

"I was frightened Daniel, terrified. I'd broken the law, I'd put others at risk. I felt sure I'd be put in prison. Finally the zoo called the police, said I hadn't been into work for several days. They broke down the door, made a terrible mess. They found me lying on the floor, I won't try and describe the condition I was in. When I got to hospital they took one look at me and then sent me down for an operation. When I came round my arm was gone."

In the silence that followed Daniel could hear the clock ticking. His grandad was miles away. Eventually he started speaking again.

"I was lucky. The zoo didn't prosecute. They said I'd been through enough. They even kept me on at the zoo doing what jobs I could with my one arm. But it was like wearing a badge of guilt and everyone could see the result of my stupidity."

"I think it sent me crazy too. I couldn't do anything for the war effort. I just moped about feeling sorry for myself. And it was then that I started to believe that the war was wrong. I've always hated the idea of killing anything. As a lad I never got my fun from jumping on slugs or pulling the legs off spiders I found that I couldn't agree with our country going to war. Too many people would be sure to die."

"I should have kept quiet, kept my head down and got on with my life. But I didn't. I went to meetings where there were others like me who couldn't face the thought of killing anyone. They called us "conchies" short for conscientious objectors. Everyone else was there because they refused to join the forces. The daft thing was that nobody would have let me join up. With my one arm I'd have been too much of a liability

Daniel heard his grandad give a half-chuckle. "Kelly's grandad was out there doing his bit, fighting for his country. When he came back he wouldn't let it rest. He and his mates used to threaten me. I was a coward in their eyes. They had no time to listen to me. It's him who's told Kelly, you can bet on that."

The old man shivered. His face was drawn and it looked as if the effort of reliving a painful part of his past had taken everything out of him. "Daniel, turn up the fire will you, I'm suddenly feeling really cold."

Daniel hardly heard him. He was deep in his own thoughts. He found that his legs were taking him towards the door. He needed to be by himself for a while so that he could think things out. Was his grandad a coward as Kelly said or had he honestly believed that Hitler could have been stopped without bloodshed?

As he closed the door of his grandad's flat he heard him call out, "Daniel, you will come and see me again?"

****

Usually on Friday nights Daniel packed a bag and caught the bus to stay with his mum for the weekend. This weekend would be different. His mum was away on a course to do with her job as a secretary. As he left his grandad's house Daniel headed home, conscious all the while that he might well be a target for Kelly's gang.

When he went to bed that night, his head was spinning. There were so many problems to grapple with. Why were his dad and grandad so obsessed with snakes when all they seemed to have brought them both was pain and suffering? Why did his grandad act the way he did? Was he a coward as Kelly's grandad claimed or had he really believed that the war was wrong? One thing Daniel knew for certain, he had to stop the Horton gang broadcasting the news about his grandad all round the school. But how?

In the early hours of the morning when Daniel finally drifted off into a troubled sleep, he'd made one decision. It was a decision that would at least show Kelly and her mates that he was no coward. He would go and look for them, and when he found them he would find some way of stopping them spreading the news. He didn't know quite how he'd manage it and he knew that he'd be putting himself in great danger, but he felt better for having made the decision.

Chapter Six

Daniel didn't have to search too far for the Horton gang on Saturday morning. He spotted them from his bedroom window. They were gathered in the recreation ground at the back of his house, and they were amusing themselves by preventing smaller children from using the swings. He watched them for a moment. It was almost as if he'd wished to find them and hey presto, his wish had come true.

He thought briefly what a shame it was that more pleasant wishes didn't come true like that. Each Saturday evening his dad sat waiting for the lottery results and Daniel would be wishing too that the right numbers would come up. One of Daniel's daydreams was that a huge win on the lottery would enable them to buy two houses, one for the family and a second for the snake. Then his mum would never have to worry about the creature being in the same house as her. They'd all be together again. Reluctantly he turned his thoughts back to Kelly Horton. What was he going to say to her?

He grabbed his coat, left the house and opened the back gate. He skirted the old entrance to the air raid tunnels and headed across the grass towards the gang. They stopped swinging and stared at him. Kelly was the first to speak.

"Well, well, who'd have believed it? Look what we have here girls. He must want more of what we gave him the other day."

"I don't believe it," said Louise. "He's after something

but it's not that."

"Who on earth in their right mind would want more of what we dish out," said Dolly. "Let's see what he wants, this could be interesting."

"What do you want, coward?" boomed out Selena.

Daniel paused about ten metres from the gang. He looked round. With a bit of luck he could make it back to his garden before they caught him if he had to. Surely he'd practised enough with Errol. It would depend, as Errol always said, on a powerful start.

"I want to talk to you."

"Go on then, talk," called Kelly, "We do sometimes let people talk before we clobber them, but you'd better have something interesting to say because we get bored very quickly. We might want to carry on where we left off the other day."

Daniel cleared his throat. "I want you to stop saying that my grandad was a coward. It's not true."

"Oh yes it is. My grandad fought in the war. All yours did was to shoot his mouth off telling everyone that they shouldn't fight. He was a coward all right."

"I think you should know both sides of the story, not just what your grandad says. He never liked mine, he was always picking on him."

"Isn't it funny how history repeats itself," said Kelly, "now we're picking on you. That's neat, I like that."

"Can we start picking on him again now Kelly, I'm tired of talking." Louise was always impatient.

"In a minute. Anyway, you must take after your grandad because you're always running from us. You're just as much a coward as he was."

Daniel clenched his fists. He had an urge to launch himself at them and inflict what damage he could yet he held back. He was certainly no kamikaze pilot. He liked to believe that there was some real chance of survival before he did anything rash. They must be right about him.

Louise wasn't the only one who was getting impatient with Kelly. The gang didn't understand her tactics. How she liked to play with her victims, like an angler plays with a fish, before landing it and dealing a death blow. Kelly got up and began to walk towards Daniel. The others followed. Daniel turned and moved back several paces. He saw the entrance to the old tunnels in front of him and an idea hit him.

"Wait," he said.

"We're not waiting any longer."

"If you were really brave, you'd want to show other people how brave you were. It's not bravery to gang up on someone and tear them to pieces. I don't think you're any braver than I am."

He thought that he'd gone too far but Kelly held back the others. He spoke again.

"If you were really brave you'd take a walk down those tunnels."

The girls laughed. "We've done that" said Dolly. We've done that hundreds of times, that's easy."

"But you haven't been down there at night," said Daniel, "when the ghost of that German pilot is on the prowl."

"What German pilot?"

"Didn't you do World War Two with Mr. Metcalfe last year? Surely he told you about the German pilot who crashed his plane on the school grounds?"

"He may have done. I can't remember. I had too many other things to think about."

"Well, that's where he's haunting, I bet you."

"What do you mean?"

"Well somehow the pilot pulled himself out of the

wreckage before it blew up. And somehow he made it across to the tunnel entrance in the school grounds. When they found him he was lying at the foot of the steps in a crumpled heap. It wasn't the crash that killed him, it was the fall."

"How do you know that's true?"

"My grandad told me," Daniel said with fingers crossed behind his back. "He used to work down the tunnels making sure everyone was OK. Now if you really want to show that you're brave you'll get yourselves down there one night and ...."

"We'll do it," said Kelly. "Won't we girls?"

Daniel didn't detect any real enthusiasm from Louise, Dolly or Selena. In fact they looked rather shocked at what their leader was getting them into.

"We'll do it," continued Kelly. "But with one condition."

"What's that?"

"It's a double dare. You go down there too, with your mates. We'll see who runs first."

"Agreed," said Daniel with rather more enthusiasm than he felt. How could he now persuade Errol and Paul to go with him. Errol had already made it quite clear that he didn't fancy a rendezvous with the airman.

"So when do we go?"

"Tonight, of course, " said Kelly, "No time like the present. We can get in through this entrance here. We'll meet you at eleven O'clock. Don't be late, and Danny boy, this had better not be a trick of some kind. You be there or else."

"I'm not a coward, I'll be there. And if you run first you can stop saying that my grandad's a coward. OK."

"OK. But there's no chance of that. We won't be running anywhere. I intend to interview this ghost."

As Daniel turned and walked back towards his garden

he heard Louise's voice, "You're not going to let him go are you Kelly? Can't we have a bit of fun with him first?

He heard Kelly's reply too.

"Look it's a dare, right. We show them what it takes to be brave and then we give them a good kicking, or maybe something more, depending on what you girls have in mind."

****

When Daniel returned home he noticed that there was something different about the place. It took him a minute to realise that the room was tidy. His dad must have had a bit of a spring clean before he went out. The ironing board was missing along with the pile of un-ironed washing that always covered an armchair. Magazines and papers were tidied away and it looked as if the hoover had been dragged round the room. Daniel cooked some toast and concentrated on eating it without spilling crumbs on the floor. What was up, he wondered, would someone be calling round, someone his dad wanted to impress?

He took his plate back to the kitchen and discovered that he'd missed a note by the kettle.

Daniel, back about two. I'm bringing someone round to look at the snake. Keep the place tidy, Dad.

Daniel didn't particularly want to be around if his dad was heading up to the loft.

In his bedroom he sat thinking. Usually on Saturday afternoons he'd be down the town deciding what to buy with his pocket money but he would have to forego that pleasure this week. He desperately needed a plan. He thought up a number of ways in which the Horton gang might be made to look foolish but dismissed them as unworkable almost immediately. By the time he heard his dad's key turn in the lock, Daniel was beginning to think that he might, just might, have the glimmering of an idea. But first of all Errol had to be persuaded to join him, he knew he couldn't do it on his own, and then possibly Paul, if he wasn't too scared of what the gang might do to him.

He heard voices downstairs.

"Do come in. I don't think the place is too untidy, unless Daniel's had his friends round, then we could be faced with anything."

He heard a woman's laugh. For one brief moment he thought his mum had come back but when she spoke his hopes were dashed.

"Nice enough place Pete, how long have you lived here?"

"Quite a while now, more than ten years in fact, we moved in soon after Daniel was born. Had a poky little flat before that, quite useless with a baby around."

Daniel moved quietly out onto the landing and peered down the stairs. The hall was empty. He crept down a couple of stairs until he could see into the living room. The woman had her back towards him.

"How about tea before we check out the snake?"

"That would be lovely, thanks."

She moved out of his line of vision and Daniel guessed that she'd crossed the room and was looking out of the window.

At that moment his dad appeared in the hall, "Daniel, are you in?"

Daniel tried to pretend that he'd been on his way downstairs, but he could see that his dad suspected something. The stairs had always been a good place to discover what was going on between his parents. Late at night when he ought to have been asleep he'd often been woken by loud voices. He'd heard some terrible rows between his mum and his dad, always the same problems - his dad's job and the snake upstairs. His parents had begun to find him huddled up and cold, clinging to the bars of the banisters. Now he simply felt foolish.

"Daniel, come and meet Rachel. She's just started work at the reptile house and I promised to show her my pet."

When she turned round, Daniel could see that Rachel was younger than his dad. She wore jeans and a jumper, her hair was frizzy and she had a nice smile. She walked towards him and held out her hand.

"Hi, I've heard a lot about you."

Daniel was taken aback. He'd heard somewhere that you should always give a confident hand shake but he seemed to take no part in this one. He felt his hand being lifted up and down but felt that he had no control over his grip. He wondered what his dad had been saying about him. She went on,

"I'm not surprised that you don't like snakes, to be honest, I'm not too keen on them myself and I have to work with them. I much prefer lizards. You know where you are with a lizard."

"Not with a chameleon," his dad said, as he brought the tea through. "You just think that you've sussed out a chameleon's behaviour and he changes colour. Chameleons are like people, full of surprises."

Daniel wasn't really taking in what was being said. He was still staring at Rachel. She was looking at his dad. Did they really just work together or was there something else?

His dad seemed nervous. The teapot always poured badly and his dad was making a terrible mess on the tray. She walked across and touched his arm. "I 'll do it Pete."

Daniel noticed the look that his dad gave her and how his fingers touched the back of her hand as she set a cup down beside him.

If Daniel ever found himself thinking how one day his dad or mum might meet someone new and want a divorce, he pushed the thought aside. He was desperate to know that a way would always be open for his mum and dad to get back together again. So how serious a threat was Rachel?

Daniel sipped his tea and said nothing. His dad kept smiling at both of them. Rachel broke the silence, "It must have been tough for you both these past few months."

What did she mean "tough". Daniel felt angry. He'd had no choice. This was the way his dad had chosen to play it. If it was tough for him, serve him right. And what had his dad done to make it easier for him? Precious little. He hardly ever found the time to do anything with him. He said he was always tired or always working. Sundays too. Daniel had a sudden thought. "How many of those Sundays had he really been working? Perhaps he'd been spending all his time with.....this woman." Daniel wanted to stop thinking of her as Rachel.

The next thing that his dad said made him really mad.

"After we've seen the snake, what about something to eat? There's a place about five miles along the coast, does a reasonable meal. Do you want to come Daniel?"

Did he want to come? Did his dad think that he'd seriously want to have tea with his dad and some substitute for his mum? No way.

"No, I'm not hungry."

"Well what are you going to do then, while we're gone?"

So this was his dad trying to show his new woman that he was really concerned about where Daniel was. Half the time he couldn't be bothered to ask. As long as Daniel appeared in the house of an evening or came down to breakfast in the morning, that was all that seemed to bother him. Where he went or who he was with didn't seem to be of any interest. He couldn't remember the last time that his dad had asked him what he'd done all day.

"I might go over and see grandad."

"You'll have to wake him up first. He'll be snoozing in front of the telly on a Sunday afternoon. Anyway Rachel, if you've finished your tea, let's go and take a look in the loft and then we can get some food."

Rachel looked down as she passed Daniel's chair, "It's been good to meet you Daniel, I hope I see you again."

"Not if I see you first," Daniel muttered under his breath.

He heard his dad set up the loft ladder and pictured him helping her into the loft. Perhaps if his mum had taken a little more interest.....but she was probably frightened, just like he was, and it was fear that drove her out. A fear that was strong enough to make her agree to give up her son. It wasn't her fault, it was his dad's. He hated him for bringing round some other woman too, and he hated her for being there, in the loft with his dad.

A few minutes later Daniel left the house and hurried towards the town centre. It was a strange sort of progress, cautiously moving from street to street, carefully looking round each corner to check that the Horton gang weren't around, then sprinting as fast as he could to the next corner. After ten minutes or so Daniel walked through the door of Barhampton Library. It was a slim chance but they just might have what he needed.

Chapter Seven

When the church clock finished striking eleven, Daniel, Errol and Paul left the safety of Daniel's back garden and moved round to the part of the old tunnel entrance where with a bit of twisting and turning it was possible to slip through into the darkness. All three boys carried torches and were dressed warmly.

Fortunately Paul had been staying at Errol's house for the night while Errol's parents were at a party. "Loo Brush will look after you both," his dad had joked. Errol reckoned it would be twelve-thirty at least before his parents returned. Daniel had found it trickier to escape the house but his dad had returned about ten, sat down to watch the football and then fallen asleep in the chair. As soon as he heard the sound of snoring, Daniel collected his shoulder bag and sneaked out without waking him, but he was fifteen minutes later than the agreed time.

Errol had been complaining to Paul for the past quarter of an hour and rounded on Daniel once he appeared. "I don't know why I let you talk me into this. I must have a screw loose. To go down the tunnels with a bunch of female vampires tagging along is suicide. If we don't get out of here alive I'll kill you!"

Daniel chuckled, "If we don't get out of here alive then we'll all be haunting these tunnels till kingdom come."

"What's in your bag?" Errol asked.

"Best if I don't tell you," said Daniel. "If you're tortured you can't reveal any secrets."

"Ssh" whispered Paul, "I hear voices."

Kelly and her mates were making their way across the recreation ground and as they drew nearer it was obvious that they hadn't really prepared for the trip. They were wearing thin jackets and disco gear. They'd obviously been partying somewhere and had left in haste to keep the appointment. Kelly had a shoulder bag with a torch inside but Louise, Dolly and Selena could only find a key ring torch between them.

"You still want to go through with this?"

"Of course," snapped Kelly, but the other three didn't look quite so certain.

It took a while before everyone had managed to squeeze through the gap in the brickwork and was standing at the top of a large, wide flight of steps that led down into blackness. They paused to listen for any noise but heard nothing apart from the dripping of water somewhere close by. There was a rusty handrail at the side of the steps and everyone clung to this as they inched themselves down one step at a time. The route was treacherous. Chalk debris lay everywhere and in places the steps were broken. It would be only too easy to trip and plunge headfirst.

They reached the end of one flight of steps and turned a corner to find a second flight, narrower this time but again spread with chalk and flint. No one was talking, everyone was too busy concentrating on reaching the foot of the steps without twisted ankles.

A tunnel led off from the steps. It was about two and a half metres high and a metre and a half wide. The walls were a mixture of chalk and flint with jagged lengths of iron sticking out every now and then. Fortunately these were mostly above head height. Daniel guessed that they'd probably been used for hanging lamps.

"OK ghost," Kelly called, "we're coming to find you. Hope you've got the kettle on."

The other girls laughed. Kelly liked them to laugh at her jokes and they always tried to do what she wanted.

The torches were throwing their shadows onto the walls, long distorted shadows rather like the effects you see in a Hall of Mirrors. Their legs looked as tall as telegraph poles. Quite soon they came to a part of the passage way that had been flooded. Daniel's grandad had told him that it was water seeping through from the surface but the girls were worried. They boys had worn boots and they were delighted to find that Kelly's gang were wearing open toed sandals.

"I ain't going through that," said Dolly. "What if it gets worse?"

"We get wetter, dear Dolly," said Kelly. "Get your shoes off and roll up your jeans."

The water did get deeper and at one point it was halfway to their knees. As they splashed through Dolly kept on moaning how cold it was while Louise and Selena just looked at each other and kept on wading. It was no good arguing with Kelly, they knew better than that. Far better to go along with her and then she couldn't complain.

At one point the tunnel divided. "This way," Daniel pointed, "This'll take us under our school." Whenever he went down the tunnels he remembered the Greek myth where Theseus found his way through a maze of underground tunnels in search of the Minotaur, a fearsome beast, half-man, half-bull. No one else had ever found their way out of the maze but Theseus unwound a ball of thread as he went along and once he'd killed the Minotaur he was able to find his way back. Daniel didn't think he'd need a ball of thread in these tunnels but he was always careful to note which direction he was taking and to reverse it on the return journey.

They turned another corner and discovered a fall of

chalk that they needed to clamber over. There was only about a metre of space between the floor and ceiling at one point. Kelly called out to Selena, "Whatever you do Selena, don't shout. A voice like yours could bring these tunnels crashing round our ears."

Both Errol and Paul looked really worried at this point. "It's not far now," Daniel whispered.

After another five minutes or so Daniel shone his torch into a side passage where there was a narrow flight of steps. "My guess is that these steps lead up to the trapdoor in the school corridor. I'm going to take a look."

He disappeared around a bend and the watchers below heard nothing for several seconds till finally there was a series of knocks. Then Daniel reappeared, "Just as I thought, it's blocked, they'd have had to block it off with children around. Tell you what, we've seen nothing so far, let's wait here for a while and be quiet. Turn the torches off for a bit and let's save the batteries"

For a few minutes they sat in silence, then Daniel announced that he needed to pee and disappeared up the steps for a second time.

"We're not going to see anything anyway," said Kelly, "It's a waste of time. We missed the last hour of our party to go tramping around down here, and for what? I don't know why I let you talk me into this, we should have just bashed you up there and.........."

Kelly didn't finish her sentence. From the darkness ahead came a voice, a loud voice, a foreign voice.

It sounded very much like a German voice.

Nobody else said a word, but the girls were holding on to each other and Errol felt sure they'd stopped breathing.

Next moment Daniel clattered down the steps and raced past them.

"I saw him he shouted, I saw the ghost."

"Quick, switch the torch on." Kelly's voice

"No!" a scream of terror, "Leave it off, I don't want to see it."

"For heaven's sake turn it on, let's see what it is. Shine it up the steps."

"No, I'm off."

"So am I."

"And me!"

Louise, Dolly and Selena, with only the key ring torch between them, were racing down the tunnel and away from the voice as fast as they could go. Kelly was still backed up against the wall, her torch shining up the steps but picking out nothing. The three boys had retreated now and were watching too. Surely Kelly wouldn't want to face up to whatever she thought was ahead of her.

But Kelly moved forwards, up the steps towards the voice. Was she really going to look round the corner and face whatever might be lurking there. Daniel had to admit it, she had guts.

She disappeared from sight. The voice stopped. Daniel knew they'd been found out.

"Good try guys, but not good enough," Kelly reappeared. "A cassette player, and a Teach Yourself German tape from the library. Now let me think Danny boy. You must have had this in your bag and set it going when you went to pee."

Kelly's voice was icy, " I repeat, good try, but not good enough. I believe these belong to you."

Daniel moved to collect his gear but Kelly dropped it on the floor. He stooped to pick it up and she armlocked his head. She brought her face up really close to his and then hissed, "If you ever try anything like that on me again I'll finish you off, do you understand?"

Daniel was having trouble getting his breath. Errol and

Paul seemed frozen to the spot unable to help him. Kelly pushed her knee into Daniel's back but he twisted free and gave her a shove which sent her sprawling on the ground. He snatched up his things and ran. He heard feet pounding behind him and hoped it was Errol and Paul.

Halfway back to the entrance he found Kelly's gang huddled together and shaking with fear. He yelled at them, "Move, it's coming this way."

The girls wailed loudly and stumbled along behind him until they reached the pile of chalk. With remarkable speed they clambered over the top and down again, then waded through the water.

Finally they all reached the steps and raced up them, tripping and stumbling over loose chalk and stones. They found the gap in the brickwork and squeezed through. They stood panting.

After a time Louise asked, "Where's Kelly?"

"Last time we saw her she was trying to snog the ghost of that German pilot," said Errol.

"What's all that?" asked Dolly, pointing to the gear that Daniel was carrying.

"Oh that, I just found it in the tunnel."

The girls looked puzzled. "But what shall we do about Kelly?"

"That's your problem, we're going home."

They left the girls peering into the tunnel entrance and calling to Kelly.

"It was a good idea," said Paul. "Pity it didn't work."

"One thing's certain though, we'll catch it tomorrow. Kelly Horton will be on the warpath. It won't be safe for any of us to go out." said Errol.

Daniel was quiet. How could he face the kind of public broadcast about his grandad that Kelly would be sure to deliver at school on Monday?

Chapter Eight

It was quiet when Daniel woke next day. There was no noise from downstairs and when he looked for his alarm clock he was surprised to find it was nearly 11 o'clock. He struggled out of bed, remembering with dismay the events of Saturday night. He needed to do some thinking.

Downstairs there was a note on the doormat

NOBODY TRIES TO MAKE A FOOL
OF KELLY HORTON.

He screwed up the note and threw it in the bin. It was nothing new, he'd worked that out for himself at the moment when Kelly discovered his trick. He didn't feel like breakfast so he opened the door and went outside. The road was empty. He'd have to risk the Horton gang.

Sometimes, when he was on his own, Daniel enjoyed pretending he was part of an SAS unit. He'd move from cover to cover, watching for snipers and keeping his eyes open for the first signs of a hostile army. He used these tactics now, crouching down behind hedges, moving from parked car to garden wall, always alert for movements or voices which would warn him that the Horton gang were close by. Fortunately, on this occasion the gang must have been terrorising elsewhere and he was able to reach his grandad's flat safely.

He rang the bell. There was no reply. He rang it again, longer this time and put his ear to the door. After what seemed like ages he heard a door open and a voice call out "I'm coming."

When the door opened, his grandad peered out. He had obviously just shaken off sleep and was looking rather confused. "Oh, it's you Daniel. I don't usually get visitors on a Sunday. Come in."

The old man continued, "I really didn't expect to see you after our talk last week. I thought that you didn't approve of me. I felt I'd let you down. But it wasn't like that, you know."

"What do you mean, grandad?"

"Look, you sit yourself down and I'll make a drink. There's a bottle of coke here, do you want some?"

"Please."

"Have you eaten? I've got an apple pie somewhere, had a bit yesterday. I'll cut you off a piece."

"Let me do it."

"No, I'm OK. I've lived without this arm for over forty years now. There isn't much I can't do. Your grandma tried to do everything for me but I never let her. I even used to climb ladders to fix the guttering. She used to tell me I was a fool. I suppose I was, I was stubborn too. I'd get to the top of the ladder and somehow manage to tie a belt round me and the ladder, bit like a harness, and there I'd stay till I'd done what I had to do. Couple of times I nearly fell. She used to go on something rotten but you know Daniel, I'd give anything to hear her going on at me again right now."

Daniel ate his apple pie while his grandad seemed lost in his memories.

He looked around the room. It wasn't much of a place to wind up your life in. A one bar electric fire gave off a little heat but away from the fire it was chilly. It was gloomy too. His grandad coughed.

"Daniel I've got to tell you this. I've thought of nothing else since you left the other day. I've got to tell you the full story because you'll hear it sooner or later, and I rather suspect it will be sooner if this Kelly girl starts talking to her grandad again. You see, he won't stop at calling me a coward and in his eyes I was a traitor too."

"How do you mean grandad?" Daniel felt awful, surely there couldn't be more.

His grandad lowered his voice to a whisper, "That Jerry pilot, the one who crashed on your school field, I saved his life Daniel, or more accurately, I helped to save his life. But according to Kelly's grandad and his chums I should have let him burn."

The room felt even colder. Daniel shivered. His grandad had paused for a moment, then he continued.

"It was on a night when there had been heavy bombing raids for a month or so, and the day before there'd been a bomb on the butchers in the High Street. Several people had been sheltering there under the butcher's tough wooden table. They hadn't had time to make it to the tunnels. The siren went and the bombers were on us immediately. Ordinarily they'd have been OK, but it was a direct hit. No one survived. Everyone felt dreadful about it.

"The next night they were over again although there were no casualties. Then just after the all clear, the warning siren went again. I was up top fire watching. I was stationed in your school grounds. There were no bombers this time just a couple of stray fighters taking a look at what damage had been done. The ack ack guns got one of them and the next minute I saw he was coming down. I thought he'd hit the houses but at the last minute he straightened out and put the plane down in the school grounds. It was either a sheer fluke or brilliant flying.

"The flames were all over the plane and I felt sure that the pilot would burn with it. I got up as close as I dared but it was hot as a furnace. Then I saw the cockpit lift and the pilot struggling to release himself from a tangle of belts. He was a young lad, hardly twenty and I just couldn't stand and watch, I had to help.

Then just at that moment I saw someone else making for the plane and I knew from the strange way that the figure was moving that it was Jimmy Dixon. You won't know about Jimmy Dixon, Daniel. He was what everyone called a 'loony'. He wasn't quite right in the head. He must have been about eighteen or so and his mum still took care of him. But he hated shelters and even in the thickest raid you'd find him wandering around in the open.

"I called out to him but he didn't take any notice. As we got closer the heat was terrible and I knew that we'd be fried too if the fuel tanks exploded. The next thing I knew young Jimmy was right by the plane with the pilot. Somehow I managed to hand the pilot my knife and he cut the belt that was trapping him. Then he stumbled clear, fell from the wings and lay on the ground.

"His clothes were alight and I beat at the flames with my greatcoat. I tried to pull him with my good arm but he was unconscious and an awful weight. Then Jimmy was alongside me. He was a big lad and he seemed to have the strength of a cart horse. We dragged him towards the tunnel entrance and I don't know Daniel, but somebody was watching over us at that point because we'd just put a bit of a distance between ourselves and that plane when there was an almighty explosion. The Jerry groaned after that and opened his eyes. Somehow he got the idea that we had to get moving and he got on his feet. We stumbled and fell the rest of the way and then finally reached the steps.

"That was when we were seen by those who had been taking shelter, or rather I was seen. Once he saw a crowd on the tunnel steps Jimmy just melted away. I knew why.

Crowds were bad news to Jimmy. He'd been taunted and ridiculed by crowds in the past. I didn't blame him for keeping clear. But as for me, I clung onto this Jerry and shouted at them to help me but no one moved. Then Kelly's grandad pushed his way forward, it was just my luck that he happened to be on leave from the army. I can still remember his first words, 'Let's hang him, he said, let's string him up.' "

"I don't know whether Hans or Fritz or Heinrich or whatever his name was, understood English but the hostility towards him was pretty obvious. He clung on to me, as if I were his only friend, and he wouldn't let go. Kelly's grandad told me to get clear of him but I didn't move. He'd picked up an iron bar from somewhere and he waved it at the Jerry. "He should have let you burn mate, but as he didn't it's up to us to decide your fate. I say we hang him."

"The mob behind him cheered and other voices took up the chorus, 'Hang him, hang him, hang him.' "

"Well the pilot was trembling. He held up his arms and I heard the word 'surrender'. Kelly's grandad kept ordering me to get away but I stayed put, desperately trying to think of the right words to try to reason with the baying pack that he was leading. If they had swept me aside and dragged the pilot off, they would certainly have hanged him.

"So I said to them, If you want our pilots to get this treatment when they are shot down, then you carry on. How would you feel if it was your husband or your son or your brother who was hung from the nearest lamp post? Don't you realise that the RAF are doing the same thing to German cities each night?"

"Whether my words would have had any effect or not, I can't tell, because just at that moment the pilot tried to make a run for it, but he must have missed his footing on the steps. He toppled over and crashed down the first flight. Nobody moved to help him at all and he just lay there whimpering."

"Fortunately a police van showed up pretty quickly after that, and an ambulance soon afterwards. They took a stretcher down but the Jerry was in a bad way, fractures as well as burns I reckon, I don't think he was even conscious any more when they took him away. And of course, we never heard what happened to him."

"I'd said nothing about Jimmy Dixon's part in all this. They hadn't seen him and I certainly didn't want anyone chasing after him. I could see that the crowd were in the mood to give anyone a beating.

"I was about to get off too when Kelly's grandad came up to me, 'Perhaps we should make do with coward here,' he sneered. 'But he's not just a coward, he's a traitor. I bet he's wired up a transmitter and is sending messages to his German friends. I vote we search his house.' "

"This idea went down well with the rest of the mob and they surged across the field in the direction of my house. I charged along after them and found them breaking down my door. I was powerless to stop them. They wrecked the place of course, and found nothing. No one apologised. They just trooped off and left me to pick up the pieces.

"But I did the right thing Daniel, I knew it then and I know it now. And if I was a traitor because I wasn't like the rest of them, because I still had some respect for human life no matter what the nationality, because I still had respect for law and order and for decency, then I'll happily accept that label. But I was no traitor Daniel. We saved that man's life, Jimmy and I, and I'm proud of my part in it."

Chapter Nine

Mr. Metcalfe disliked Monday mornings. He disliked Monday mornings because they came round far too frequently. They also meant that he had a whole week of teaching in front of him, another whole week with 6M. At 8.45 a.m. on a Monday morning he could always be found in one of the staff room armchairs cradling a cup of coffee and dreaming about what might have been. He played the Lottery each week and spent a lot of time thinking about what he would do with a big win. His favourite Monday morning dream was of a Caribbean cruise. He'd be lying on the deck, putting some serious effort into his sun tan, while the wine waiter brought him exotic cocktails. That would be the life.

"Hello Mike, I thought I'd find you here," Mrs. Francis breezed into the staff room. "I must tell you this, I was in the checkout queue at the supermarket on Friday evening and I suddenly realised that Mrs. Humphries was in front of me. You know her Mike, don't you? Mother of Gareth in 4C. Well, we chatted for a bit and then she asked me about this ghost story. Apparently all the parents are discussing it at the school gates.

"It is really rather ridiculous when you think about it. Are they seriously suggesting that we have a spectre in full flying gear patrolling the corridors of this school after dark?"

"I don't know what they're suggesting at the moment, but I do know that at 8.15 this morning I arrived to find the phone ringing. When I answered it I had a reporter from the Barhampton Gazette asking me to 'fill him in' on the ghostly rumours about our school. I was rather sharp with him and he certainly didn't get the quotes that he was looking for. Now he'll probably write something pretty awful about us anyway. We must do something to knock this rumour on the head."

"What do you suggest?"

"Well, I had a plan on Friday, and then over the weekend I thought it wouldn't work, but now I think it just might."

"Do you want to tell me about it?"

"I don't think I will at the moment, if you don't mind, and then if it backfires there'll be no one to blame except me. Hope you don't mind being kept in the dark on this occasion?"

"What can I say, you're the boss!"

Just at that moment the whistle was blown in the playground. Mr. Metcalfe groaned, "What have I done to deserve 6M?"

"You know you love them really!"

"Oh yes, every last one of them. Still, they're not a bad as last year's bunch. Remember Kelly Horton and her band of brigands. They're at it again, you know."

"At what?" Mrs. Francis looked puzzled.

"Boy bashing. It's what they do best. The lads are terrified of them, they'll try any trick to delay leaving school at night. I discovered from listening in to conversations, that this gang of Kelly's lies in wait for the boys on their way home from school and then pounces. The lads have all sorts of horrible things done to them."

"Why hasn't anyone complained?"

"They daren't. If you were a boy, would you complain that you'd been beaten up by girls? And aside from that, they know they'd get it again, and worse."

"Shall I speak to them?"

"You could try, but I can't see the Horton gang changing their ways. They enjoy what they do too much. Anyway I'd best get along there now before there's a riot to quell."

"Well Mike, there's not much we can do about them now, they're beyond our control. But do let me know if you hear anymore about our ghost. We must put a stop to that one."

****

When Mr. Metcalfe reached his classroom he knew that something was up. Little Carly French was on sentry duty and immediately scuttled inside calling "He's here, he's here..."

"Good of you to announce me Carly."

Out of the corner of his eye Mr. Metcalfe noticed that all was not well with Daniel Palmer. He was laid out flat on the floor and pinned down by Kelly Horton's knee on his chest. Kelly still hadn't realised that her former teacher was in the room, she was far too busy explaining to Daniel just what she proposed to do to him as a result of his trickery in the tunnels.

"And when I've finished with you," she shouted, "You won't even recognise yourself. You'll look like something from a horror film, something that's been buried for years and has just been dug up. You'll look like......" She paused mid sentence as it dawned on her that the room had gone quiet. She looked round.

"I would be most grateful Kelly, said Mr. Metcalfe, "if you would get off of Daniel and let him get up please. I've no idea what you're doing here when you should be in your own school. You'd both better come here and tell

74

me what's caused all this."

"If you tell him anything Daniel Palmer," Kelly growled, "I'll do what I'm planning to do to you twice over. Have you got that?"

Daniel nodded. They both stood in front of Mr. Metcalfe's desk and nothing he could do or say could persuade either of them to talk about what he had just seen. "We had a disagreement at the weekend," Kelly said looking sulky.

"Right, we've wasted enough time, I'll see you later Daniel. And Kelly, you'd better get back to your own school. I shall be ringing up later to tell your form tutor just what you've been doing."

All in all Daniel had a pretty miserable day. He knew that Kelly wasn't bluffing. She'd do everything she said, and worse. He dreaded home time, she was sure to be waiting for him. During silent reading he appeared to be deep in his book but really he was praying for a miracle.

Daniel always felt that he missed out when it came to miracles happening and so he certainly wasn't pinning any hopes on a rescue. But at three-thirty when he could delay leaving school no longer, there in the playground he found his mum. She was wearing a long black coat that he hadn't seen her wear before, and she'd changed her hairstyle. She was smiling too and she looked well.

"I missed you at the weekend," she said. "I thought we could go into town and have a chat."

Later on, when he thought about it, he felt guilty about his feelings at that moment. He was pleased to see his mum, that was true, but she didn't realise how pleased he was. Her timely visit, whatever the reason, would now save him from the Horton gang's clutches. Errol and Paul were quick to take advantage of the situation too, and they walked along with Daniel and his mum, until the Horton gang grew tired of shadowing them and moved off in search of easier targets.

After they'd said goodbye to Errol and Paul, they walked towards the town centre. Daniel's mum wanted to know how he was doing at school and how his dad was coping. He thought it best not to mention that his dad could well be seeing someone else, he wasn't sure how his mum would react and he didn't want to spoil his time with her.

They went into a coffee shop and his mum bought him a milkshake and a doughnut. They talked again about school and then his mum grew quiet for a while. Daniel licked his sugary fingers and sipped at his milkshake. He wasn't prepared for what his mum said next.

"I was thinking that maybe your dad and I ought to give it another try."

Daniel couldn't believe what he'd heard. Half of him wanted to jump into the air like Fred Flintstone does shouting 'Yabba dabba do' while the other half remembered his dad's friend, Rachel. That couldn't happen now. It mustn't happen now, just as his mum had said that she might come home again.

His mum must have seen his worried expression. "What's the matter Dan, don't you want me back?"

"Yes, of course, more than anything," he said. But what could he say? Should he mention Rachel? Did his mum already know? And that wasn't all that was worrying him. What about the snake? The situation hadn't changed. It was still there in the loft. An unseen presence, a threat.

"What about the snake Mum? I thought it terrified you too. I thought that was why you left?"

"It was, I know, but I just feel now that maybe I overreacted. After all, your dad was very careful with the creature. I know I could never understand why he wanted to keep it in the house. Maybe your dad couldn't understand me when I used to go on and on about Elvis, all those scrapbooks I had when I was a teenager, and still have now. I knew all his songs too, off by heart. I suppose that was my obsession."

"Anyway, we're going to get together, your dad and I. We'll meet up one evening and see if we still argue as much. We won't rush. Anything that happens will have to be gradual. Don't get your hopes up too much, but we will be heading in the right direction."

****

Daniel's mum left him at her bus stop. It was only a short distance to his house but his head was spinning with the thought of what his mother had just told him. Would his dad feel the same though, would he want what she wanted. And what could he do to help things along?

As Daniel turned a corner by the gasworks he was ambushed from behind. He was pushed to the ground and his hands pulled tightly behind his back. He felt his arms being tied together with string and a piece of cloth was wound round his eyes. How could he have been so stupid? He'd been so caught up in thinking about his parents that he'd forgotten to be on his guard. He'd offered himself up to them, like a sacrifice.

He heard their voices, taunting, mocking and felt their hands roughly lift him up and propel him in the direction they wanted to go. If he stumbled or hesitated he felt a kick to his legs or bottom.

"You're going to regret that you ever dreamed of trying to trick me, Daniel Palmer. No one gets away with a stunt like that, no one."

He tried to guess where he was being taken but it

wasn't a long journey. He was pushed against something and felt hard ridges dig into his back. He stood there gripped in a tight hold while he felt more string being wound round his arms.

"That'll do," Kelly's voice again, "you can let him go now."

He tried to pull away but he couldn't move his arms. He was securely tied to something and there was no possibility of releasing the blindfold.

"You know we could have had a lovely time together Daniel. We tried being friendly towards you but you didn't like our kisses. Shall we try again? Does anyone still want to snog this little rat?"

Daniel was horrified, but no one answered Kelly. Louise, Selena and Dolly were still too unsure of Kelly to risk saying the wrong thing. They'd been in deep trouble too for abandoning her in the tunnels on Saturday night and now they waited for their leader to tell them what to do.

"I'm very glad that you didn't all rush because we're going to bid a tearful farewell to Daniel now and see how long it takes Mr. Houdini here to escape from his chains. Come on girls. Oh I forgot, we could kiss him goodbye."

Daniel twisted his face away, moved it from one side to the next, but he still smelt hot bubblegummy breath and felt wet lips too close to his own.

Then it was quiet.

The string was hurting his wrists. He felt the hard edge of what he supposed were railings digging into his side. They hadn't come far from the gasworks and he rather suspected that they'd tied him to the black railings around the recreation ground. That would please them, imprisoning him so close to his home.

The pain was bad now. What made the whole situation

doubly bad was that he couldn't see a thing and he had no way of removing the blindfold. He strained his ears to hear if anyone was passing close by. After a couple of minutes he heard footsteps, "Help me," he called out, "help me, please." But no one came and he heard someone running away.

How long he remained there he couldn't begin to tell until he heard the church clock strike eight o'clock. Almost an hour he reckoned. He was cold and stiff. The pain in his arms was intense. He didn't know how much more he could take.

"What the hell..... What's been done to you lad." A gruff voice, rough hands untying the string, pulling away the blindfold, releasing him. He felt wobbly and collapsed in a heap on the ground. "Thank you."

He recognised the man as a regular dog walker on the recreation ground, and he obviously recognised Daniel, "You live round here, don't you?"

"Yes, number 39."

"Who did it? I think I ought to speak with your parents."

"I'll be all right really, it was a joke that went wrong."

"I'm not sure I believe that. I'm still coming home with you, come on."

Daniel walked ahead of the man and was relieved to find no lights on when he came to his house. "I'm OK really, I'll let myself in, I've got a key."

"I'm not happy about this. Perhaps I ought to ring the police, I'll see. Are you sure that you're all right?"

"Yes, thanks again, goodnight."

Daniel escaped indoors and then sank down into an armchair. He was shaking and pretty soon he found that he was crying too. He felt hungry but he hadn't the strength to fix himself something to eat. He tried to clear his head, to focus on how he really felt about his mum, his dad, his grandad, but it was all too much of an effort. He lay back and closed his eyes. When his father came home a couple of hours later he found him asleep in the chair.

Chapter Ten

Daniel's dad was concerned about him the next morning. "Are you sure you're OK," he asked him. "It's not like you to fall asleep in the armchair."

He even asked Daniel if he wanted to take the day off school. Daniel was very tempted but he knew how bored he'd be just moping about the house all day. Finally his dad went off to work and Daniel was about to call on Errol when he heard the sound of his letterbox. On the door mat he found a message on a crumpled piece of paper.

WE WANT TO SEE THE SNAKE.

There was no doubt where it had come from. All his friends knew about the snake in his loft but every time they'd asked to see it, Daniel had turned them down. He looked out of his window to see Kelly staring at his house, her face fixed in what she must have thought was a smile, but for Daniel it was more like a leer from an evil witch. He screwed up the paper again and dropped it on the floor.

The letterbox clattered again and he jumped. Another screwed up ball of paper was on the mat. He flattened it out and read the message:

IF YOU DON'T SHOW US THE SNAKE WE'LL GIVE YOU
THE SAME TREATMENT AS LAST NIGHT.

Daniel shivered, he certainly didn't want a repeat of what happened then, but he absolutely refused to be press-ganged into giving them what they wanted, And besides, he couldn't bring himself to go up in the loft and meet the creature face to face. Kelly really would see him trembling and she'd know for certain what a coward he was. He would have to think of something, some way of distracting her, but what?

A third piece of paper dropped through the door.

TONIGHT, AFTER SCHOOL,
WE'LL WALK YOU HOME.

Daniel opened the door and stepped outside. Kelly was leaning on the gate.

"Leave me alone."

"We have no intention of leaving you alone Danny boy. What you had last night was merely the start. You see Daniel, you and your mates need to understand that if anybody tries to trick me, they'll get what they deserve."

"But if I show you the snake you still won't leave me alone, will you?"

"Let's just say Daniel, that we'll go easy on you. I can't be fairer than that."

"Oh yeah," he laughed, "You'll just tie one hand to the railings instead of both of them."

"Something like that."

"Get lost."

Daniel headed back indoors. He had a feeling that he'd just said something foolish, something that would bring the Horton gang after him once more. His thoughts were interrupted by a fourth piece of paper that confirmed his suspicions:

YOU WILL BE SORRY.

At this moment Daniel's main worry was how to get to school without the Horton gang offering him an escort.

The front way was useless, he could still see them all through the window. He called Errol first and then slipped out the back door, down the garden and over the fence into the recreation ground. Errol was waiting for him.

"I saw them too," he said and then sprinted down the field. Daniel sprinted too and for once he managed to keep up with Errol.

****

Towards the end of the morning, Mrs. Francis called in and looked round at the work they were doing. Daniel was finishing off some illustrations of what life was like in Britain during World War Two. She asked him a few questions about this and then moved on. Later he heard her talking to his teacher. They were speaking with their voices lowered but he managed to make out what they were saying.

"Mr. Matthews, one of our school governors is very concerned about what he's been hearing. Parents have phoned him to complain and although he thinks the whole idea is nonsense, he's requested a governors' meeting to talk it over. He thinks that if the word gets round too much, then true or not, we'll end up losing children to other schools."

Mr. Metcalfe sounded amazed, "Surely not. Surely an intelligent man like he is can't believe that this school is haunted?"

"I don't think it matters whether he believes it or not Mike. But what does matter is that other people seem to think that there's some truth in the story. We need to convince them there is no ghost."

"Yesterday you said that you had an idea. Have you managed to sort it out yet?"

"Yes I have, I've made a couple of phone calls and so far I'm very pleased with the results. You could say that everything is going according to plan and that I hope to have an answer to the problem in a matter of days."

"That will be a big relief. Then we can go back to being the school that is known for its football results rather than its ghost!" Mr. Metcalfe paused, "There would, of course, be one sure-fire way to check out the story, you know."

"And what would that be?"

"Well, we could hold this governors' meeting at midnight, get everyone in one night and do a spot of amateur ghostbusting!"

"If I thought that you were serious," said Mrs. Francis as she moved towards the classroom door, "I'd be very worried about you."

Mr. Metcalfe smiled, then suddenly realised that half his class were looking in his direction

He coughed. "OK, back to work."

****

Daniel spent most of the day trying to think up a way to outwit the Horton gang. He certainly couldn't rely on a second miracle, he knew that he'd had his quota for months to come. He thought about pretending to be ill and hoping he'd be sent home. Then he realised that the school would have to phone his dad at the zoo and he'd have to take time off work. He'd probably insist on bundling Daniel along to the doctors and Daniel wasn't sure if he could keep up the act for quite that amount of time. There were no clubs after school that he could temporarily join and Mr. Metcalfe didn't encourage anyone to stay and help tidy up. In fact Mr. Metcalfe's classroom was pretty untidy for much of the time but it didn't seem to worry him.

At lunchtime he told Errol about the problem but he had no answers. "Well Daniel," he said, "I'd like to help you out but....I'd quite like to stay alive too."

Towards the end of the school day Daniel was no nearer to finding a way out of his dilemma. He found it hard to concentrate on anything and Mr. Metcalfe told him off for fidgeting on two occasions. "I don't think you've just got ants in your pants Daniel Palmer, you've got a whole nest of termites!" Huh! thought Daniel. Did he really think he was being funny?

As they were collecting their coats from the cloakroom Errol came up to Daniel. "Look," he said, "I've been thinking."

"What with?"

"Hey, if you're going to be like that you can get out there and face the Horton gang on your own."

"You mean you were about to say you'd come back with me?"

"Yes, I was, but now....."

"Errol, I'm really sorry, I didn't mean it, you're brainy, you're intelligent, you're witty, you're handsome, you're......do I need to say more?"

"A little more perhaps, I was beginning to enjoy that."

"You will help me then?"

"Yes. It'll be like General Custer at the Battle of Little Bighorn." Errol loved to read about the Wild West. "A few brave men against the might of the Indian nation."

"What happened to them?" Daniel asked, "Did they win?"

"No, they were squashed, just like we're going to be. I must be mad. Lead on, let's get this over with."

****

Just beyond the school gates the Horton gang were waiting.

"We're glad that you've decided to be sensible," said Kelly. "We can have a nice stroll back to your place now Daniel, then we can take a look at your little snake."

Daniel realised at this point that Kelly had no idea how big the creature was. He wondered if she would be scared of it herself once its full size was revealed, but then dismissed the idea almost immediately. He couldn't imagine anything frightening Kelly.

"Now that we've got these two lads here, it does seem a pity to waste the opportunity," said Louise. "I never did get to give Daniel a snog."

"Not now," barked Kelly, "we have more important matters to attend to. But I'll tell you one thing," she turned to Daniel and Errol, "If either of you two are thinking of tricking me again, I'll be happy to let Louise loose on you."

"You see we've been looking up the world record for snogging in *The Guinness Book of Records,*" said Dolly. "Are you ready for this? The world record stands at seventeen days, ten hours and thirty minutes and when they'd finished, they both had to be taken to hospital and given treatment for lip blisters."

Daniel and Errol looked at each other. It was a stupendously frightening thought. Perhaps the Horton gang were in training for an attempt on the world record. Well they wouldn't be practising on them, they'd make sure of that.

It took about fifteen minutes to walk from school to Daniel's home. It was a distance of just over a mile and Daniel always thought that it was quite a long way, especially in the rain. On this occasion it would have suited Daniel if the journey had been five times as long. He felt just the way he always felt when his mum used to take him across town to visit the dentist. He never wanted the journey to end. But Daniel thought that any number of trips to the dentist would be preferable to this journey.

The girls had formed a tight ring around Daniel and Errol. If they slowed then Selena behind them would tread on their heels. If they moved out of line then Dolly or Louise would be there to encourage them back again. And Kelly, up front, was setting the pace, alert for any trouble behind her.

Soon, too soon for Daniel, they turned into his street. Kelly stopped. "You'd better be sure your dad's out."

Daniel hoped against hope that his dad might have come home early for one reason or another. Then they could escape indoors and leave the girls on the pavement. He knew that there wasn't much chance of that, and anyhow it would only be putting off an inevitability. Kelly wanted to see the snake and what Kelly wanted, Kelly got. He knew that.

Daniel stood at his door, key poised. He knew he'd be in dreadful trouble if his dad found out. But he had no choice, you just didn't say no to the Horton Gang.

"Dad," Daniel called out, but he knew before the sound of his voice had died away that the house was empty. You can always tell an empty house, it feels different. It reaches out to pull you inside, and even though everything is familiar, you can often feel a little uneasy.

"Don't hang about on the doorstep, let's go and look." Kelly and her mates pushed past him and into the hallway. Daniel thought that in the past his house had always been somewhere to escape to. Now he would never be able to look on it again in that way. The enemy had broken down his defences, and what made it worse was that they'd broken them down without a fight being put up.

"Right, where's the ladder?"

Daniel pointed to the top of the stairs where there was a cupboard that contained his dad's newly acquired extending ladder. The girls pushed and pulled the ladder into place.

"Hey this snake isn't sliding around loose up there, is it?" Louise sounded worried. "Because if it is I'm not going to be the one to take out that hatch." She backed away.

"It's quite safe," Daniel said. "It's in a glass cage, like you see at the zoo, and providing you don't mess with the bolts, that's where it stays."

"Right, let's go then." Kelly looked round to see if anyone else was volunteering to go first. No one moved. Daniel was still hanging back on the stairs but Errol was pressing forward. He had always wanted to see the snake and now he'd got his chance. So that was why he'd been prepared to risk the Horton gang.

"You go first Daniel, you know what to do."

Little did they know. He had never done this by himself, would never dream of doing it by himself. Reluctantly he moved towards the ladder and began to climb. He listened for any sound that might indicate that the snake was active, then pushed gently against the loft opening. The hatch moved a little, enough for Daniel to peep through.

"Do you always keep a light on in your loft Daniel?"

"Yes, we have to. It's a special sort of light that gives out heat. The snake has to be kept warm or it won't survive." Daniel hoped that his voice wasn't giving any indication as to how scared he really was.

He could see that the snake was asleep. That was good. Perhaps now they would be satisfied just to take a look at the creature and then get down again. Kelly was pushing against his feet, "Get up there Daniel, I want to look."

He climbed into the loft and off the ladder, keeping it

between him and the snake. Kelly climbed up after him, "Wow! Ain't you a beauty, a real beauty. How long is it Daniel?"

"About three and a half metres."

Kelly made way for Louise, Dolly and Selena to follow her and by the time Errol made it to the loft it was getting rather crowded. Still the snake slept taking no interest in her visitors.

"Is it poisonous?" Selena asked with a voice that reverberated around the loft.

"No, it's a constrictor. It coils itself round its victim and squeezes till whatever it has caught stops breathing."

"Hey Louise," called Kelly, "that's just the way you like to do things."

"Funny."

"So could we feed it Dan, I'm really interested you know." Who did Kelly think she was kidding. She'd gone closer to the snake and pushed her face up against the glass.

"I'd be very careful if I were you Kelly," said Errol. "If that snake wakes and sees your face it'll be frightened to death."

Daniel stopped breathing, why on earth did Errol have to go and say that for. They'd be for it now.

But Kelly didn't seem to hear, she was absorbed in the snake. "It's the most marvellous creature. Look at the markings, what an amazing pattern. I wish I could feel it. I always thought that snakes were slimy to touch but they're not. We went to a zoo last summer and there was a snake handler there who draped one of these things round my neck. It felt really smooth and warm. Oh it's lovely Daniel."

Kelly sounded almost human, almost friendly. Daniel couldn't believe it.

"We ought to go down now. My dad will kill me if he comes back and finds us all up here. This is out of bounds for me as far as he's concerned."

Louise, Dolly and Selena all looked as if they'd had quite enough and were about to go down but Kelly wouldn't budge. She was looking at the snake from every angle. Suddenly there was a movement, a slow uncoiling. The snake lifted up its head and looked straight at Kelly. "Wow!" she breathed, "I do like you."

Chapter Eleven

"Daniel, isn't it time you went to bed?"

His dad was home tonight. He'd arrived home shortly after Daniel had finally managed to persuade Kelly to leave the snake alone and get out of his loft. Then he'd had trouble getting the ladder back in the cupboard. Errol hadn't stayed to help. He'd shot down the ladder and out the front door. Presumably he'd been worried for his own skin when Kelly stopped being hypnotised by the snake and started thinking back to what he'd said about her face. Daniel had just made it down to the living room and switched on the TV when he heard his father's key in the lock. His father had been very cheerful. He had told Daniel to switch the oven on to warm up some fish and chips which he'd picked up on the way home.

All the way through the meal his dad had ignored the TV and asked him questions about what he'd done at school and how he was coping. Daniel began to wish that he'd be his normal self, sticking his head in the paper or watching the News. Then he changed the subject.

"I've heard from your mum. She says she's spoken to you. She wants to see if we can try again. How do you feel about that?"

"You don't really need to ask, do you dad. It's what I've always wanted I miss her, I've never stopped missing her."

His dad looked thoughtful. "I miss her too son."

He got up and cleared away the remains of their meal.

Daniel spent the evening finishing off some work that he had to do for school. It was something he would usually have completed in lesson time if he hadn't spent all day worrying about Kelly.

When his dad called out that he ought to be getting to bed, he collected a drink from the kitchen and headed up to his room. He lay in bed reading for a while and then there was a ring on the doorbell. He strained his ears to hear who it might be.

It was a woman's voice, one that he'd heard before, fairly recently. His dad hadn't told him that she'd be coming round. No wonder he'd been in a good mood. And all that stuff about missing his mum, it can't have been true. He listened to the voices downstairs. They rose and fell and were punctuated with occasional laughter. He resented her being in the house, this Rachel who seemed to have taken the place of his mum, as far as his dad was concerned.

Before she arrived he'd felt guilty about letting the Horton gang into the house, but now he swept aside all thoughts of guilt. Serve his dad right. Why should he feel guilty about going behind his back? He'd do it again too, if necessary, if that's what it took to keep the Horton gang from picking on him. And again, and again, and again. Anything had to be better than being tied to the railings for a second time.

****

"Daniel."

It was the following afternoon and Daniel had almost reached home. He had just been congratulating himself on avoiding the Horton gang's clutches and he had his front door key in his hand.

"Daniel, stop a minute."

Kelly Horton was on her own. There was no sign of the

rest of the gang. Daniel stopped, "What do you want?"

"Can I see the snake again?"

"What's in it for me?"

"We'll leave you alone."

"How on earth can I be sure of that? You will all the time it suits you and then when you're fed up of this, you'll start up again."

"Please Daniel. That creature's magic. Please let me see it again."

He wished that his friends could have heard this. Kelly Horton was pleading with him, she was actually begging him to do something for her. This was a totally different side of Kelly, one that he'd certainly never met before. He thought back to the events of the previous evening. His dad and Rachel, together. And this morning he hadn't said a word, he'd just gone off to work as usual. Well he would let Kelly see the snake once more if it would benefit him, why not?

Daniel opened the door. "Just a quick look this time, all right?"

"Yes, anything."

This was certainly a new side to Kelly Horton. He could see that she was excited at the thought of seeing the creature once more. She steamed in through the door and without pausing headed for the stairs. By the time Daniel had reached the cupboard where the ladder was kept, she'd taken it out and heaved it into place. She climbed the ladder, pushed back the trap door and disappeared from sight. Standing at the foot of the steps Daniel could hear her talking to the snake. It was a strange sort of talk, half crooning, half singing. "She's flipped," Daniel thought to himself, "she's gone completely mad." He wondered if he should tell her that snakes don't have ears in the way that humans do, although the creature would probably be picking up the vibrations from her voice.

He climbed the ladder and saw that Kelly had her arms out to the snake. She leant forward to cuddle the corner of the glass where the snake was curled. It was unbelievable. If anyone had said to Daniel that one day he would find Kelly Horton in his loft whispering sweet nothing's to a three metre long snake, he would have told them they were out of their minds.

After ten minutes or so, Daniel began to get worried. He didn't feel too guilty about deceiving his dad but he didn't want to be caught doing it.

"You'd better come down now Kelly, my dad could be back at any moment."

He expected to have to keep on at her but she came away immediately. Again he couldn't believe that Kelly Horton was doing something he told her to do, and doing it meekly as a lamb. She didn't say anything as she eased herself back down the ladder leaving him to close the hatch. When he caught up with her in the hallway he saw that her face had a look of contentment, an expression he'd never seen before.

At the door she paused, "I want to feed her."

"You can't, it wouldn't be safe."

The expression on her face changed. She advanced towards Daniel. "I said, I want to feed her."

"You can't. You need to take proper safety precautions. You can't just open the cage and throw something in."

"I can Danny boy, and I will." The old Kelly Horton had returned now. He had backed against the wall and she had moved very close to him, her face close to his. "Do you remember Daniel, the last time we were as close as this?"

Daniel remembered only too well.

"If you don't let me feed her then Louise, Dolly and

Selena will do their worst with you, after I've had a chance of course."

Daniel shivered. He knew that this was no idle threat. He'd have to agree.

****

It had just struck 7 o'clock on St. Mary's Church clock and Mr. Higgins, caretaker at Barhampton Primary School had finally finished locking up for the night. He was looking forward to a meal and an hour or two in front of the television. He was just turning away when something caught his eye. He looked again and felt certain that he'd seen the glow of a light from inside the building. There were no cars about and no other lighted buildings nearby so he was sure that it couldn't have been a reflection. He had been school caretaker for the last nineteen years and had learnt never to ignore a gut feeling. At this precise moment something was telling Mr. Higgins that he wouldn't relax for one moment if he didn't open up the school again and do a thorough check.

He fitted his key in the lock on the side door that he always used to exit from the school, and he turned it very quietly. The lock was well oiled, he always saw to things like that, and the key turned silently. The hinges didn't squeak at all as he opened the door and stepped inside. He closed the door behind him and stood on the doormat listening. There was no doubt about it, he could hear voices. The nearest telephone was in Mrs. Francis's room and he trod lightly in that direction. There had been a number of school break-ins recently and Mr. Higgins was no hero. The police could deal with them.

Mr. Higgins spoke softly into the telephone and was told that the police would be with him very shortly. He stood by Mrs. Francis' door and listened again. The voices were closer this time and a beam of light was travelling along the corridor outside. He looked for somewhere to hide and decided on the cupboard where Mrs. Francis hung up her coat. He stepped inside and closed the door. As his eyes grew used to the darkness he noticed an umbrella. He gripped it with his right hand and prepared to use it as a weapon if he was forced to.

Moments later Mr. Higgins heard footsteps and realised that he was trembling. Voices sounded from the corridor outside Mrs. Francis's office.

"You can't go in there, that's her office. We'll be in real trouble if she finds out we've been poking about in there."

"We must look in there. We came back to search the place from top to bottom, so it's got to be a thorough search. We won't get the chance again."

"Yes, we must look everywhere." A girl's voice this ime.

Kids. School kids. Mr. Higgins smiled grimly. He was lieved to discover that he wouldn't have to tackle rglars. They must have sneaked in before he locked up. He'd have them, he'd give them a shock. And what were they looking for anyway?

Suddenly it dawned on Mr. Higgins. They were looking for the ghost, that Jerry pilot who crash landed outside. Of all the nerve. He would find out who they were and report them to Mrs. Francis in the morning.

He heard noises, They were inside the room now and without any warning whatsoever the cupboard door was flung open. It was hard to tell who was more shocked. Mr. Higgins at least was half prepared for what he saw but the four faces that were suddenly confronted with a very angry school caretaker registered shock, disbelief and absolute one hundred per cent terror. Mr. Higgins was no German pilot but he was totally unexpected and the ghost hunters were temporarily frozen to the spot.

Mr. Higgins was the first to recover. He emerged from the cupboard brandishing the umbrella, "What do you think you're doing?" he roared.

Nobody stayed around long enough to answer him. They fled, and as Mr. Higgins chased them into the corridor a police car complete with flashing blue light drew up in the driveway outside. There was no hope of catching the kids, Mr. Higgins knew that, but now he'd have to spend time testing all the doors until he found the one that they'd escaped from. It was at times like this that he hated kids. And what on earth would he say to the policemen that he'd summoned?

****

Mrs. Francis looked grim. Assembly was almost over when she said that she had an important announcement to make.

"Last night," she began, "there were four children in this school when they should not have been here. They sneaked in when Mr. Higgins was occupied elsewhere in the school."

A murmur went round the hall and Mrs. Francis waited for the noise to stop.

"Coming back to school in the way that these children did was a very foolish thing to do. They could have been locked in all night. They might have been injured and nobody would have known. It was only due to the prompt action of Mr. Higgins that the children were discovered."

She paused to let her words sink in. "I don't know who the children were. Mr. Higgins caught a glimpse of them but I do not propose to hold an identity parade. I would just ask the four children responsible to come and see me after assembly, and I do expect to see them. I hope I've made myself clear. In the meantime, no one is ever, and I do mean ever, to try and pull off such a stunt again."

Mrs. Francis turned and left the hall. A buzz of excited chatter started up while the teachers called for silence. On the way back to their classroom four children left their class line and headed off in the direction of Mrs. Francis' room.

****

"Mr. Metcalfe, may I have a word please?"

Mrs. Francis had come into the staff room at lunchtime and interrupted Mr. Metcalfe's lunch. He made to get up from his seat."

"Stay where you are, I'll just grab a coffee and then I'll join you."

A few moments later she sat down, "I've had a very interesting conversation with those four children who visited last night. They're dead set on this ghost existing and they furnished me with a list of all possible hiding places around the school. That's what they were doing, checking out all the possible locations."

"And did they find anything?"

"Mrs. Francis laughed. "Only a very angry caretaker hiding in the cupboard in my room."

"What was he doing in there?"

"Oh don't ask me. I think Mr. Higgins is quite embarrassed about the whole episode. He's already done his explaining twice over, once to the police and then again to me. Anyway, what I wanted to say was that I had a letter this morning from a friend of mine in Germany. He thinks that he will be able to do what I've asked him to do."

"And what's that?"

"Well he's attempting to trace the pilot to check if he's still alive. It's a long shot I know, but if I can get a letter from the pilot himself, I can read it to the children and knock this ghost idea on the head."

"I wish you the very best of luck," Mr. Metcalfe replied.

Chapter Twelve

A piece of paper dropped through Daniel's door, another postal delivery from Kelly Horton.

TONIGHT, I'LL WAIT FOR YOU.

It was a few days since Kelly had warned Daniel that she wanted to feed the snake. Daniel had begun to think that she might have lost interest but he should have known better. In the playground he tried to talk to Errol but he'd chosen a bad time as Errol was deeply involved in a game of football. It looked to Daniel as if there were two football matches criss-crossing each other. Errol appeared to be playing for two teams at once, booting whichever ball came his way. Daniel managed to get close to him when the action had moved to the other end of the playground, but it wasn't a good time to interrupt.

"Just listen to me a minute, will you?"

"Oh come on Daniel, I've helped you out in the past but if you've got involved with Kelly Horton then I'd rather stay clear."

Errol moved quickly to trap a ball as it came in his direction. He booted it away again.

"Look at it this way," Daniel started again, "If I'm doing what Kelly wants then she's out of your way. You ought to be thanking me."

"I do thank you Daniel, I do, but if I didn't know you better I'd be thinking that she's become your girlfriend."

Daniel made a lunge for Errol but he side-stepped and

set off after a football. When the action moved on again he strolled back to where Daniel was standing.

"Take it back," snapped Daniel.

"Take what back?"

"That bit about Kelly being my girlfriend."

"Oh that, I was joking."

"Well will you help me then?"

"Help you with what?"

"She wants to feed the snake. I need someone to raise the alarm if anything goes wrong."

"You must be off your head. You mean you're going to let Kelly open up that snake's cage while you stand and watch, and you want me there. I'm not going anywhere near that creature if it's likely to get loose."

"It won't get loose, I promise you. I know what to do."

"Well, *if* I come, and I'm still not saying I will, I'm not getting into that loft. I'll stand at the bottom of the ladder, and don't expect me to hang about waiting for a huge lump of snake to drop on my head. No thank you. I don't mind looking at the creature when it's safely locked away but I'm not about to become fast food for a python. No way!"

"And I'll tell you something else," Errol went on, "If Kelly Horton so much as blows a kiss at me, I'm off. I just don't like the sort of creatures you hang around with, they're both reptiles."

With that remark, Errol turned and chased after a ball. Daniel smiled. He knew that despite everything, he could rely on Errol. He'd be there.

****

"Daniel, take a look in here."

It was lunch time but Kelly Horton must have walked

out of her school and was paying a call on Daniel. She was in the playground and holding out a carrier bag.

"What is it?"

"Just take a look will you?"

Daniel looked. Inside the bag were two dead rats. Kelly was smiling, "I did well, didn't I?"

"Where did you get them?"

"The tunnels. Carl went down there with me. We took his air pistol and picked off several." Carl was Kelly's brother and an even nastier piece of work. He'd probably taught Kelly all she knew.

"I got into dreadful trouble," Kelly went on. "I wrapped the rats up and stored them in our fridge overnight, I wanted them to keep fresh. Trouble was that my Mum unwrapped them this morning thinking they were fish that dad had brought home. You should have heard her scream. We didn't need an alarm clock, mum's shrieking woke everyone up. Dad flung them out into the garden but I went and got them back once everything had calmed down."

Daniel couldn't help smiling at the thought of what had taken place in the Horton household.

"So will they be OK?" Kelly asked.

"Should be. But we'd better stick with one. I don't know how long ago Dad fed her last. She might not be hungry, snakes don't eat like we do."

"What do you mean?"

"Well, this one only feeds every ten days or so. I'll have to check on the calendar, dad always marks the days when he feeds her. If she's been fed fairly recently she may not be interested in what you're giving her."

"We can only try Daniel, and we're trying tonight. All right?"

"I just hope you know what you're doing."

****

102

Daniel couldn't believe his eyes, or his ears for that matter. He and Errol had just left school and outside on the pavement the Horton gang were laying in to each other. This was wonderful to see and a crowd was collecting round them. As far as Daniel could make out, Kelly's position as gang leader was being challenged by Dolly, Louise and Selena. They were complaining that Kelly had lost interest in the gang, all she ever talked about were snakes.

"You and that wimp Daniel Palmer," Louise shouted. "You don't care about us anymore."

"We don't see why you should be leader, one of us could do a much better job." That was red rag to a bull as far as Kelly was concerned. She twisted round, wrenched hold of Selena's hair and pulled her head towards hers. With a moan that must have been heard on the other side of Barhampton, Selena fell against Kelly, pulled herself free and then slapped at her face. The slaps must have stung Kelly but what really goaded her on was the realisation that her leadership was being challenged with everyone standing round enjoying the spectacle. She hurled herself forward, kicked out at Selena causing her to stumble and topple over.

"This is magic," Errol called. "Let's hope they tear each other apart."

It did seem for a while that they might just do that. Faces were scratched, stomachs punched, arms twisted, hair pulled out. Daniel thought about the no holds barred cat fights that he'd often watched from his bedroom window. This was certainly as violent as anything he'd seen moggies get up to. The street was filled with shouting, screaming, swearing and finally another voice, a voice of authority. Mrs. Francis on her way out to her car had heard the commotion and come to see what was happening. The

103

onlookers disappeared very quickly leaving the Horton gang to explain their behaviour.

"I think that we've just witnessed the end of a beautiful friendship," said Errol. "What a shame!"

Daniel thought that if the Horton gang were no longer a force to be reckoned with, they would all be able to breathe more easily, but he didn't think it would finish as simply as that.

When they reached Daniel's house he invited Errol indoors. They poured some cola and switched on the TV. When the doorbell rang, Daniel wasn't really surprised, just disappointed. He had hoped that Kelly would have forgotten about snake feeding in all the kerfuffle that had taken place. He got up and went to open the door.

Kelly looked a wreck. Her coat was torn, her face scratched, and it was obvious to Daniel that she had been crying. A few days ago he wouldn't have believed it possible that her granite features could ever have squeezed out tears. Now he almost felt sorry for her. She pulled the sleeve of her coat across her face and sniffed.

"I've lost them." she said sadly.

Daniel thought that the loss of friends like Louise, Dolly and Selena could well be a matter for rejoicing, not tears. But then he supposed that if they were the only friends you'd ever had, it would still be quite a shock to lose them.

"Someone took them," Kelly went on, "I put them down when the fight began and someone stole them. And now I can't feed her."

Slowly it dawned on Daniel that it wasn't the loss of her friends that was upsetting her, but the disappearance of the two rats that she'd been carrying about in her bag all day. He felt immediate relief.

"It wasn't a good idea Kelly, believe me," he said. "My dad would have known that the snake had been fed by someone. He always goes up to check on her each evening, he never misses. He would have seen the bulge in her throat. It takes hours for the meal to be digested. He would have known that I'd been letting you see the snake and that would have been the end of that. I tell you, if you want to go on seeing her then you'd better forget about feeding her."

Daniel didn't know whether what he said had registered with Kelly or not, but if she couldn't do what she wanted to do, she at least wanted a consolation prize.

"Please let me see her again Daniel."

He held the door open and she stepped inside, "This can only be a quick visit, my dad....."

"I know, don't worry."

They followed the usual procedure and once Kelly was installed in the loft Daniel and Errol waited at the foot of the ladder. They heard her talking to the snake. It was awake this time and showing an interest. They heard her telling the snake how much she wanted to stroke her and they heard other sounds and noises, the kind that people make to babies or cute kittens. Errol looked up at the loft opening then put his finger to his head and twisted it. "She's crazy," he whispered, "get her down before she does something really daft."

"It's like this each visit," Daniel answered. "Who'd have believed it?"

"Not me, that's for sure. If you'd have told me this yourself I'd have thought that it was you who'd gone gaga."

Just then Kelly's head appeared. She sounded excited. "Hey, I've thought of a way that we can feed her. We've just got to do it in the morning so by the time Daniel's dad goes to look at her, she's digested her meal and what she's swallowed can't be seen."

Daniel looked at Errol. "That's no good," he said, "I'm not here at weekends, I stay with my mum."

"We won't need a weekend," Kelly went on. "It's half-term next week, we can do it then."

"I'm not so sure Kelly, I told you I don't think it's a good idea."

Kelly scooted down the ladder remarkably quickly for someone as heavily built as she was. "You'll agree Daniel, won't you?" she said, moving towards him in a threatening manner.

"I haven't got much choice, have I?"

Something like a smile spread across Kelly's face.

"I'm glad we understand each other Daniel."

Chapter Thirteen

Half-term brought something of a mini-heatwave, the perfect sort of weather for spending time at the beach or out in the country. Daniel stayed with his mum for the weekend but was back with his dad at the start of the week. He hinted to his dad that they might have a trip out somewhere, just the two of them. Daniel's dad had groaned and told Daniel how busy he was and how impossible it was to take time off work right now. He even had to work on Whit Monday because they were short staffed at the zoo and expecting huge crowds. His dad had given him a free pass and told him to have a look round the zoo.

That was really the last place Daniel wanted to go but in the end he went along. His dad met up with him for lunch but about half way through their meal in one of the zoo restaurants, who should appear but Rachel. His dad acted casual and pretended that it was just a coincidence but Daniel reckoned that the meeting had been planned. He finished his meal quickly and although he answered Rachel's questions politely enough, he couldn't wait to make his escape.

The zoo offered him few surprises, he'd spent many days wandering around on his own, but his dread of snakes had always prevented him from visiting the Reptile House. On this occasion he decided to prove to himself that he could face up to his fears and so he boldly marched inside. He still couldn't bring himself to go right up to the exhibits in the way that lots of children were doing. They were pressing their noses up against the glass while on the other side were the thick coils of a huge boa constrictor. They were tapping against the glass too but the snake seemed oblivious to the world outside.

Daniel left after a few minutes and was pleased to be out in the sunshine again. He also felt pleased that he'd managed to spend some time with the snakes although he was in no hurry to do it again. One other good thing about being at the zoo was that he was unlikely to meet up with Kelly. He felt sure that the Horton family's idea of a trip out wouldn't be a day at the zoo. They'd be far more likely to watch stock car racing or spend an evening at the wrestling. Something that involved people being knocked around in some way.

When Daniel arrived home that night the phone was ringing. He rushed inside and picked it up.

"Where have you been?"

Kelly Horton's voice. For a few moments at the zoo he'd managed to forget about her madcap plan. She didn't wait for an answer to her question.

"I've been down the tunnels again with Carl. I've got a couple of rats so I'll be over tomorrow morning."

That was typical Kelly, no how are you fixed for tomorrow morning, just simply be there, or face the consequences. Daniel thought of saying that he'd got something else on or that his father wouldn't be at work but he knew that she wouldn't leave him alone till she got what she wanted.

"My dad goes off at 8.30. Leave it an hour and come round then. But I'm telling you again, I still don't like........."

He didn't finish what he was saying, there was no point. She had put down the phone and that was that.

Daniel went out again. Two doors away he rang the bell. Errol's dad answered.

"Daniel, good to see you, come in. I don't know about you but this sunshine is good for me. You know I always write more when the sun is shining. It must be because I'm writing about the Caribbean and the sun always shines out there, or at least it always does in my memory." Daniel had read some of the stories that Errol's dad wrote. He thought they were brilliant.

"Errol's out in the garden," he continued, "go on through."

"Hi, what are you doing?"

Errol was lying on the ground peering into a crack in his garden path.

"I'm watching ants."

Errol's dog, Loo Brush, was also watching ants. Every now and then she'd stick her nose into the nest. Daniel watched a she lifted her head and shook it vigorously to try and shake off the ants that had climbed aboard.

"Hey Loo Brush," said Errol. "You're giving those ants a great fairground ride."

"Why are you watching ants?" Daniel asked.

"Because it's the most interesting thing that I've found to do all day."

"Well in that case you'll jump at the chance to come round and help me tomorrow."

Errol eased himself upright and took a look at Daniel. "I hope that this isn't what I think it is."

"It is, she's just rung me. It's 9.30 tomorrow or else, and personally I'm not too keen to discover what the or else might be."

Errol chuckled. "I think I know, and I'm not about to risk it either. I'll be there, sucker that I am. In the meantime I think I'll just get back to watching these ants."

The two boys and Loo Brush spent the next hour devising all kinds of tests for the ants that kept exiting from the crack in the garden path until Errol's mum called him in for tea. Daniel stayed too and happily tucked in to a huge helping of spaghetti Bolognese.

"Hope you enjoyed your final meal," Errol said as Daniel was leaving.

"What do you mean, my final meal?"

"Well, you don't actually think you'll have a future after tomorrow do you? One way or another you'll be dead meat."

Daniel didn't believe that Errol could predict the future but he was worried nevertheless.

****

At exactly nine-thirty there was a ring on the doorbell. Kelly pushed her way inside as soon as Daniel opened the door. She handed him a supermarket carrier bag with fresh supplies of rat meat.

"Right, let's get going."

"Hang on. I'm just going to leave the back door open for Errol."

Kelly disappeared upstairs, took out the ladder and swung it into position. Daniel followed her into the loft where he heard her talking softly. She was back in that special relationship that she thought she'd got with the creature. Daniel was disturbed to find that today of all days, the snake was active. He had hoped that it would have been sleeping so that they'd be able to throw in the rat, lock up and retreat, but with the snake awake he wasn't sure how they could do it. He wished he'd been brave enough to watch his father and see how he got round the problem.

"Kelly, I think this is too dangerous."

She turned on him, "You're just chicken Daniel Palmer,

just like your grandad. Well you go down then, leave us alone. This snake knows me now. It'll be fine with me."

"But you don't know what you're doing Kelly. Anything could happen when you open the door. You can't trust a snake, it'll never be your friend, it's a killer."

"I'll be all right, don't worry. I'm just checking out the best way to do this."

Daniel had discovered from the kitchen calendar that the snake was due for feeding in a couple of days time so he thought that it might well be interested in what Kelly had to offer.

Kelly sat by the cage considering what to do. After a while she reached out her hand and fingered the top bolt on the cage door. It drew back easily.

Daniel watched from the top of the ladder. He saw her fingers move towards the centre bolt, pause for a moment and then travel on to the bottom bolt. She drew this back too. Now there was only one bolt securing the door.

While this had been taking place the snake had been slithering around the cage. "Never underestimate a snake's intelligence," Daniel's dad had told him on many occasions and it seemed to Daniel as if this creature was just pretending to be indifferent. In reality it was watching every move that Kelly was making.

Kelly ran her fingers along the centre bolt. Very slowly she pulled it back while at the same time keeping her foot against the door to prevent any chance of it opening. She reached out her hand and drew the carrier bag towards her. When the snake had moved to a point that was furthest away from her, Kelly opened the door slightly, drew out a rat from the bag with her other hand and then pushed it through the gap. Then as the snake was moving back towards her she slammed the door shut and pushed back the bolts.

Daniel realised that he'd been holding his breath and with considerable relief he breathed again. He could see that Kelly was shaking slightly. He admitted to himself that she had a lot of nerve to open the cage.

The snake took a sniff at the rat and then left it there. It seemed more concerned with exercising, shifting and then rearranging its coils, while its head and neck travelled in a swaying motion from one side of the cage to the other. Again it sniffed at the rat but showed no further interest.

Daniel remembered that his dad had once said how you needed to be careful what food you gave to a snake. He hoped that the tunnel rat wasn't diseased in some way. Daniel also knew that if the snake refused the food, it would have to be removed from the cage, and that would be a far trickier operation.

Kelly had moved round to the far side of the cage and was trying to interest the snake in feeding, or at least Daniel assumed she was doing that. She was making the sort of noises that Daniel had heard before and the snake seemed interested. It kept coming over to Kelly's side of the cage and staring at her. But nothing she said or did had any effect. The snake continued to ignore the rat.

They watched and waited until Daniel discovered that over an hour had passed. He knew then that they would need to take the rat away. If his father came back and saw that they'd been trying to feed the snake, he'd go crazy. He knew that his father had had to remove food on previous occasions and he wished he'd asked him how he did it. Kelly looked as if she wasn't too sure whether she wanted to open the door again while the snake was still active, while Daniel knew that he was looking into the stuff of his worst nightmares.

Daniel looked around and noticed that there was a stick propped up against the cage. It had a piece of wood attached to one end making it look rather like a broom without the bristles. It looked as if it was the kind of stick that his father might use to place behind unwanted prey and hook it towards the door. He pointed this out to Kelly who began to unlock the bolts once more. Again she waited until the snake's head was furthest from the door and then grasping the stick in one hand Kelly leant back to allow the door to open a fraction.

What happened next, Daniel couldn't be certain. Kelly claimed later that it was pins and needles in her foot that caused her to topple backwards and it could have been the joist in the loft floor that caused her to miss her footing while trying to regain her balance. But whatever happened, the door opened slightly and the next moment Daniel saw the python's head in the gap followed by coil after coil of huge snake thrusting itself out into the loft.

Kelly looked horrified and Daniel thought that his own face probably showed a similar expression. Neither spoke for fear of attracting the snake's attention. Kelly tried to move away but the noise caused the snake to turn in her direction and she froze. Daniel's first instinct was to escape, to leave Kelly the problem. After all he had warned her over and over again and she'd now discovered for herself how utterly dangerous the whole idea had been. But although he was shaking and probably more terrified than he'd ever been in his life before, he couldn't just abandon her. Instead he did perhaps the bravest thing that he'd done in his life so far, he left the ladder and moved into the loft.

The snake was confused. It could sense noises from two directions and it wasn't sure which way to go. The creature was now almost clear of the cage and Daniel could think of no way of enticing it back inside. It was moving towards the loft opening and soon its head hung down from the roof space as it investigated what was down below. Its head reappeared once more and then disappeared as the undulating body slowly left the loft. Daniel could see that the snake was making good use of the ladder as a means of escape.

Gradually the whole of the snake left the loft and wound itself around the ladder till finally the snake's great bulk and the uneven distribution of its weight caused the ladder to topple over and crash to the floor. At least we're safe up here Daniel thought to himself, and in the next moment realised that although they might be safe, nobody else would be. Where was Errol? He might be round at any moment and anything could happen if he met the creature unexpectedly.

Daniel looked down from the loft opening and Kelly edged over to join him.

"I'm sorry Daniel."

"That'll do me a load of good when my dad finds out, won't it?" His voice sounded strange and he was having difficulty controlling it. "Anyway, we'd better get down from here and try to find help."

They looked down at the snake which was busy untangling itself from the ladder and heading towards the stairs. They watched as it flowed down fairly effortlessly, its huge body shifting and contracting as it pushed itself along.

Daniel held onto the edge of the loft opening and then swung out into the gap until his finger were gripping the edge and taking his weight. This left him with a fall of a metre or so. Kelly followed and they stood on the upstairs landing and peered down. There was now no sign of the snake, but Daniel did hear something. It was Loo Brush barking, barking frantically and at the same time Errol's voice.

"Hello, sorry I'm late, we all overslept this morning......"
Daniel screamed, "Errol, get out the house.
"Why, what's the........Oh my God"
Daniel could only imagine what Errol had seen.

Chapter Fourteen

Daniel was trying to think rationally but all his attention seemed to be focussed on trying to stop himself shaking. He couldn't recall ever being quite so frightened as he was at this moment. Somewhere downstairs there was a three metre long reticulated python who had just scared the daylights out of his best friend. There was no chance of getting the snake back into the loft and he couldn't imagine how anyone would be able to recapture it. His father would have to be told soon but his telephone number was in the phone book by the hall telephone. Daniel couldn't risk going down there without a clear idea of where the snake was hiding. He became conscious of Kelly's voice:

"I didn't think.... I never realised.....I'm sorry Daniel, I really am... What are we going to do?"

"I don't know, all I know is that my father is going to go stark raving mad, and I must have been crazy too, absolutely crazy to ever let you pull a mad stunt like this. I haven't the faintest idea what to do..."

Just then they heard Errol's voice from the back of the house.

Daniel ran along to his room, jumped onto the bed and reached for the window catch. He threw open the window and looked down at Errol's upturned face.

"Just what have you done?" Errol screamed at him, "We came face to face with it." He was holding Loo Brush in his arms although the dog was struggling to get down.

"Where is it now?" Daniel called.

"I don't know, I shot out as fast as I could."

"Can you look through the window?"

"No way, I'm keeping clear."

"Is the back door shut?"

"No, and don't ask me to shut it, I'm no hero."

"You've got to try and shut it," Daniel pleaded. "if it gets out of the house it could go anywhere."

"Look, just you hold tight up there and I'll go and fetch my dad. He'll know what to do."

Daniel watched Errol as he raced out the back gate and along the field to his garden. In a few moments he saw Errol's dad and then his eye was distracted by another movement. The warm sunshine outside must have proved a magnet to the snake. It began to slither out into the garden.

Daniel yelled, "Watch out."

Errol and his dad paused outside the gate to Daniel's garden and peered through cracks in the fence. They all watched as the snake moved further into the sunshine.

"Are you all right up there?" Errol's dad was calling out to them.

"We're OK, but what can we do?"

"Just stay where you are and I'll make some phone calls. The police first I think and then the zoo."

Daniel turned to look at Kelly, "We're really going to be in trouble now." Her face was drained of colour and she looked as if she was close to tears. At any other time or place Daniel would have rejoiced. The great Kelly Horton about to turn on the waterworks!

Daniel looked down into the garden again. The snake had almost pushed its way out of the house now and was heading towards the sunniest part of the garden where the grass met the side wall of the air raid shelter. This had always been a regular suntrap where Daniel's mum used to sunbathe in her deckchair. Slowly the snake adjusted its position to gain the maximum benefit from the sun's rays and then lay still. From his vantage point Daniel could get a good look at the snake. Until now he hadn't really appreciated its great size. As he watched he realised that Kelly was behind him, breathing down his neck, "It's beautiful," he heard her whisper.

At that moment Errol's Dad came running back. "Daniel," he called, "The police are coming, and your dad's on his way, he's bringing help too."

The snake was still dozing by the wall. Daniel had heard his dad say that snakes can control their body temperatures by moving in and out of the sun. After its crawl down from the loft, Daniel thought that it probably needed a while to recuperate. He judged that it might well be safe to go downstairs and try to close the back door. The snake would then be trapped in the back garden and it would surely make it easier for his dad to recapture it. He was in two minds as to whether he should rush down and rely on speed to get the door shut, or whether he should creep down cautiously and hope not to disturb the snake. He moved towards the stairs and found that Kelly was close behind him. Caution won, and half way down the stairs they paused to look over the banisters and to listen for any indication that the snake might be returning to the house. At the foot of the stairs they turned towards the kitchen and had a clear view through to the garden. The snake hadn't moved. They tiptoed through the kitchen and Daniel pushed the door closed.

The snake lifted its head at the noise. Watching through a hole in the back fence Errol saw it shift slightly. Just then there was a noise of a car approaching and this seemed to disturb it even more. Its tongue flickered in and out and it swayed from side to side as if considering its next move. Errol heard running footsteps and a policeman appeared alongside him. There was the sound of a second car, loud voices and more footsteps. More policemen appeared. The snake was clearly unhappy and it began to shift along the wall.

Daniel and Kelly were watching from the window. Until the snake started moving again Daniel had believed that all would be well when his father arrived with the other zoo staff. Surely they had dealt with situations like this before. Now to his utmost horror, he understood where the snake was heading. It had noticed a gap in the brickwork, something Daniel's dad had been meaning to close up for months and had never got round to it. Daniel had played out there too, discovering one day that the space between the bricks led through into the air raid shelter. From the shelter, steps led directly down to the tunnels. Without looking back the snake began to disappear into the gap. How on earth would they find it if it vanished in there?

At that moment Daniel realised that Kelly wasn't standing beside him. He heard a door open and then saw her racing along the garden path towards the snake. She grabbed hold of the snake's tail, anchored her feet and leant back but with one huge flick of its tail the snake was free and Kelly was spinning across the garden. She picked herself up and ran back to try again but the snake must have put on an extra spurt of speed and there wasn't much tail to hold on to this time. As the last of the snake disappeared the back gate burst open and the garden was suddenly full of policemen. Daniel rushed out to find Kelly only to discover that she was trying to get back into the house.

"A torch Daniel, I need a torch,"

"Why? Oh no you can't be serious, you're not thinking of going after it."

"Daniel, find me a torch or I'll knock you down and then find one myself."

"Well you'll have to do just that because I'm having no part in this. Just leave it to the experts."

"Daniel, for heavens sake, you know as well as I do how many kids get down these tunnels. It's half-term, what if there's anyone down there already. They're going to meet it. What then?"

"But you're mad."

"Maybe I am, but I let her out and if it finds anyone down there.....well, I couldn't live with that."

This was another side to Kelly that Daniel hadn't seen before. Presumably she could live quite happily with all the other crimes that she'd committed."

Kelly advanced on him. "Where's the torch?"

Daniel found two in the cupboard under the stairs. Kelly snatched one from him and raced out the front door. As he followed he saw her disappear round the side of the house towards the back of the shelter. She paused to check if there were any policemen about and then pushed her way in through the gap in the brickwork that they'd used on previous occasions. Daniel found himself standing there with the second torch in his hand and then, with only a moment's hesitation, he followed her into the tunnels.

****

Ten minutes later there was a screech of brakes and Daniel's father jumped out of a Zoo vehicle, closely followed by two more men who offloaded a large amount of equipment. Daniel's dad was already in the house, "What happened?" he shouted, "where's Daniel?"

"Mr. Palmer is it?" said one of the policemen, a young man who didn't look as if he'd been out of police college for long. "Now I gather you kept a snake in your loft, is that so?"

"Yes, yes, yes," said Daniel's Dad rather impatiently, "I kept it there and now it's escaped, but where is it, and more importantly, is my son all right?"

"We're trying to piece it all together," said the policemen.

Daniel's dad looked around him and saw Errol and his father in the garden. He rushed outside. "Do you know anything about what's happened?"

"Well we know that the snake has gone through into the tunnels," replied Errol's father.

"But where's Daniel?"

"He was here a minute ago."

Suddenly another of the policemen called out, "We've just had a Neighbourhood Watch report that a boy and a girl were seen pushing their way into the shelter. It may well have been your lad Mr. Palmer."

"He wouldn't," said Daniel's dad. "He's scared of snakes, he wouldn't go in there knowing the snake was on the loose. It can't have been him. You said there was a girl with him, he keeps away from girls. It must have been someone else." He was conscious of a note of panic creeping into his voice.

"Well, whoever has gone in there sir," the young policeman was speaking again, "we'd better get onto them and fast before they meet up with that snake."

Just then Errol pushed his way forward, "Mr. Palmer, I think Daniel has gone in there, and the girl is Kelly Horton."

"Right we'll deal with this sir, " said the policeman. "What we'd like you to do is to give us some information on the snake.....wait, where are you going?"

Daniel's dad waved his arm towards the two zoo

officials who had followed him into the garden, "They'll tell you all you need to know, I'm going to find my son."

"I wouldn't advise that Sir," the policeman called, but Daniel's dad took no notice. He charged through the house, stopped at the van to pick up a powerful torch and then called out to Errol.

"Come and show me where you get into these tunnels."

****

The men who made up Red Watch at Barhampton Fire Station had just returned from rescuing two boys who had clambered down a cliff face and then got stuck on a ledge. Tea was being brewed and the crew sat around a large table eating chunky sandwiches or thick wedges of cake. They were under no illusions that they'd finished for the day. School half-terms were busy times and children had a knack of getting themselves into tricky situations. Steaming mugs of tea had just been handed round when the alarm went for the second time that morning.

There were groans and hasty swigs of the hot liquid, then in a very short time the men were assembled again, their equipment checked and the huge fire engine ready to leave. This time the message had been quite bizarre. It appeared that they'd been called to locate two children, one man and a three metre long snake who had all vanished into the network of old air raid tunnels beneath Barhampton.

****

Kelly and Daniel stood at the top of the flight of steps that led down into the tunnels. There was no sign of the snake. It was cool in the tunnels and Daniel wondered whether the snake would survive in such conditions. It would be losing body heat fairly swiftly he thought, and it would probably coil up somewhere to try to conserve what heat it still had. But where should they be looking and would the creature attack them if they stumbled across it unexpectedly?

Kelly started to pick her way down the steps, "Come on, it can't have got far."

"Just be careful," warned Daniel. "It's not poisonous but it can give you a nasty bite all the same. And if it curls itself around you, you'll end up with crushed ribs, that is if it doesn't succeed in squeezing all the breath out of you."

Kelly's torch picked out evidence that other children had recently been in the tunnels. There were empty fizzy drink cans, sweet wrappers, comics and a place where it looked as if a camp had been made and a fire started. "This is why we have to find this snake," said Kelly, "before it finds someone else."

They moved on, shining their torches from side to side and into every dark corner. The light played strange tricks with the pools of water that stretched out ahead. A short distance in, a side tunnel left the main tunnel.

"Which way?"

They tried the smaller tunnel but very quickly reached a place where the roof had fallen in. They retraced their steps till Kelly stopped suddenly and Daniel collided with her. The beam of her torch picked out twin points of red. Kelly started off again, "Just rats," she whispered.

"I think we should go back a little," Daniel said when they rejoined the main tunnel. "I don't think it will have crawled this far. I think, if anything, it will be coiled up somewhere, trying to keep warm."

They entered the section of tunnel leading back to the steps and this time they definitely heard something. They stopped still and listened. It could have been anything in this subterranean world, but Daniel felt convinced that they were hearing the kind of slithering noise that a large snake would make. And whatever it was, the noise was coming closer, no doubt about that. Their torches probed the darkness and then revealed a shadow that danced along the wall, alternately rising and then falling, until suddenly the snake was there and almost upon them. Daniel could see how the snake was moving its head from side to side, perhaps looking for somewhere that it considered safe, somewhere to curl up and conserve that all important warmth.

Kelly and Daniel both moved fast. They scooted back to a slightly wider area where they noticed a ledge at head height which looked as if it might offer some way of getting out of the snake's direct path. Daniel scrambled up and then offered Kelly his hand. She found it hard to get a grip and impossible to swing herself up in the way that Daniel had done. He had nothing to hold on to while he tried to heave her up and keep his balance at the same time.

A movement from the tunnel mouth meant that the snake was in view. Kelly seemed to gain a foothold and then Daniel felt himself slipping. He relaxed his grip on Kelly's hand and with a scream she fell to the floor. Her torch hit the ground and went out while in the next second Daniel's own torch started rolling along the ledge. He just stopped it in time and shone it down at Kelly. She wasn't moving.

"Kelly," he screamed.

The snake stopped moving.

"Kelly, Kelly, come on Kelly, wake up Kelly."

He moved as far over the ledge as he dared and tried to reach her but it was impossible. He shone his torch on the snake again. It still hadn't moved but its head was bobbing up and down, probably trying to work out where the sounds were coming from. Then suddenly it was slithering again, moving across the room towards Kelly's lifeless form.

Daniel knew he should jump down and try to drag Kelly away from the snake. He knew that would be the best thing, the bravest thing to do, but he was frozen with fear. Up on the ledge he was safe, and he couldn't bring himself to risk climbing down. All his nightmare fears were crowding in on him again, all the months he'd lived with this creature in the loft above his bedroom, all the times he'd imagined it breaking free, all the horrors came flooding back into his brain and he could do nothing except hold onto his torch and watch what happened as the snake moved slowly nearer to Kelly.

And then, at the precise moment that the snake reached her, Daniel heard a noise. They would be rescued, it still might not be too late. He yelled with all the strength he could muster, "In here, quickly...."

He heard a shuffling noise and then a voice, low and mumbling:

"You'll be all right, I've got you now. You'll be all right, I've got you now. You'll be all right, I've got you now...." The same few words repeated again and again.

He shone his torch around as a blurred figure came into view.

"Watch out!" Daniel yelled, "the snake....."

His voice trailed away as he began to realise that whoever had joined him in the room was taking no notice of him. As the figure moved further into the light Daniel could see that this was a young man, rather tall and with a face that was disfigured by scars. The clothes that he wore were somewhat old fashioned and his large hands were held out in front of him. All the time, the mumbling continued, "you'll be all right, I've got you now."

His first thought was to make himself as small as possible, to try to merge into the blackness, become invisible. There could only be one possible explanation. This was the ghost of the crashed German pilot. Daniel's heart was pounding loudly and the noise seemed to fill his head. He turned away from the figure and then swiftly turned back. He felt dreadfully inadequate.

Daniel shrank back on the ledge. He shouted at the figure again, but there was no reply, no indication whatever that this figure and he could communicate in any way. All he could do was watch as the figure paused, lifted his head and stared straight towards him. Daniel saw that the lips were drawn back exposing black teeth and again heard the mumbling - "You'll be all right, I've got you now."

Daniel looked down and found that the snake had shrunk back into the shadows away from Kelly, and that the strange figure was reaching down and attempting to pull Kelly away from the danger. He seemed to have quite remarkable strength and he was concentrating hard on pulling Kelly further along the tunnel.

Daniel knew that ghost or no ghost he ought to get down and help with Kelly. He peered down to see where the snake had gone and in the beam from his torch he discovered that it was curling up next to the wall directly below his ledge.

Daniel could still hear the strange figure mumbling those same words, "You'll be all right, I've got you now," and he began to hear other sounds too. He could hear footsteps and voices, and a powerful light was shining along the tunnel. "Watch out," Daniel yelled again, "the snake, it's here."

126

At that point too, Daniel braced himself for a huge leap that would take him over the snake and towards the direction in which Kelly and the strange figure had disappeared. "Here goes," he thought to himself, "now or never." He held on tightly to his torch and then with a leap that wouldn't have disgraced an Olympic jumper, he landed heavily on the floor. He rolled over once, found his feet, and ignoring the shouts and calls of his rescuers he raced off to look for Kelly.

Chapter Fifteen

Daniel discovered Kelly a short distance away where the tunnel split in two but there was no sign of her rescuer. Daniel shone the torch all around, into one tunnel and into the other. He listened out for any noise of footsteps but all he could hear was the racket behind him as the rescue team shouted out to each other, trying to decide on the best way to recapture the snake. He shone the torch into Kelly's face and was relieved to find that her eyes were open and she was turning her head away to avoid the bright light. She groaned and tried to sit up. She rubbed her head, looked around and then back at Daniel.

"What happened?"

"You fell and hit your head."

"I remember trying to get up on that ledge before the snake got hold of us, but I don't remember anything else. Where's the snake now? How did I get out here?"

Before Daniel could find the right words to try and explain to Kelly what had happened, she jumped to her own conclusion.

"You must have pulled me out here Daniel, you must have got me away from the snake."

She paused for a moment to consider what had happened, and then spoke again. "You rescued me, Daniel. Why? Why did you do it? I've always been awful to you. You could have left me, I wouldn't have blamed you...."

The words gushed out and Daniel felt powerless to stop them. He should have told the truth, he knew that, but it was easier to let her believe her own version. He'd lived in fear of the Horton gang for so long and now it seemed that he might even benefit from this unexpected turn of events.

She continued to look at him and he shrugged his shoulders. He wouldn't actually lie and say outright that he'd rescued her, he'd just let her go on thinking that he had. And anyway she wouldn't believe what really took place. He wasn't so sure that he did either. Had he really seen a ghost? Had he really seen the ghost of that German pilot?

If he tried to explain to Kelly she'd think it was another trick of some kind. But what had he seen? He was totally confused?

All these thoughts raced through his mind until suddenly he heard a voice that he recognised breaking through all the commotion and noise behind him.

"Daniel, Daniel."

It was his dad's voice.

"I'm here dad, just a bit further along."

A bright light cut through the gloom and then his dad was with him. Daniel had never seen his dad looking so worried before.

"Are you all right?"

Daniel nodded his head. "I'm sorry dad," he whispered.

Then his dad did something that Daniel couldn't remember him doing for a long time. He hugged him, and he kept on hugging him, until Daniel became aware that his dad was shaking and trying unsuccessfully to hold back tears. He let go and wiped his eyes with his sleeve. Then he suddenly noticed Kelly. With a huge sniff he managed to control himself.

"I'm sorry my love, I didn't mean to ignore you. I was just so relieved to find Daniel unharmed. Are you OK?"

"I am now. I hit my head and the snake would have got me if it hadn't been for Daniel. He dragged me away."

Daniel's dad squeezed his arm and tried to smile. Daniel knew that he would have to confess what really happened but would anyone believe him?

"Can you walk?" his dad asked Kelly.

"I think so."

"Here hold on to my arm," said Daniel's dad. "Let's get you both out of here fast."

"What about the snake dad? I really am sorry."

"Look here Daniel, I haven't yet managed to piece together what happened but I don't think that this is the time or place. When we've got back up top and sorted ourselves out, then I'll want to know."

"What about the snake. Won't you need to help trap it?"

"No, they won't need me to deal with her. There's two experts from the zoo and a bunch of firemen. They're quite capable and she won't offer much resistance, she'll be too cold by now."

There was a huge amount of activity taking place around the snake. Daniel could see men with long sticks and tough netting. Someone else was moving a large dustbin into position. They crept carefully past the scene of the action and discovered the rest of the firemen from Red Watch alert for any trouble.

"I think you ought to see a doctor," Daniel's dad told Kelly. "Best to get that bump on your head examined, make sure you haven't done any serious damage."

They climbed the flight of steps that led to the shelter entrance. Here they discovered that the space where they had climbed in had been enlarged to enable the rescue team to pass in and out. There was an ambulance parked nearby along with a fire engine and several police cars. Policemen were moving away onlookers. Reporters and photographers stood round and then hurried into action as Daniel appeared at the tunnel entrance. They shouted out questions but Daniel's dad ignored them all and concentrated on getting back to his house. One of the ambulance crew followed to take a look at Kelly and then took her off to the hospital.

****

Daniel sat with his dad drinking tea. He was amazed at how calm his dad was. He'd apologised several times now but his dad had just told him not to worry.

"You've told me why you did it, and I understand that. What I hadn't realised was that this old Horton-Palmer rivalry was still continuing after all this time. You know how it flared up over that incident with your grandad and the German pilot, then Kelly's dad used to have a go at me when I was at school, and now this. I'm sick of it, and I'm not letting it carry on any longer."

"But what about the snake dad? Can you get it back?"

"I could get it back I suppose, but I'd been thinking for a few weeks that it might not be such a bad idea to donate it to the zoo. To tell you the truth it was Rachel who made me begin to doubt if I was wise to carry on keeping the creature at home. She told me some horror story about a snake that escaped during a gale. Apparently the high winds shifted the trap door and the snake must have been loose already."

Daniel could picture the nightmare scene only too well.

His dad continued, "I was more than a little worried about how big it was growing. Even as I was rebuilding the cage, I had my doubts about the wisdom of keeping it in the house but I suppose it needed something like this to point me in the right direction. So don't worry any more, I think you've done me a favour in one way. But don't let on I said that if the police come calling. I'm sure that they'll want a full statement soon."

"Does this mean that Mum might come back?"

"Just hold on will you, you're racing ahead. Let's just take things slowly and see what develops. I certainly haven't got as far as that yet, and anyway, even if I asked her to come back, there's no guarantee that she would. After all, I treated her badly and she's got her own life now."

It was on the tip of Daniel's tongue to ask his dad where Rachel fitted in to all this but he kept quiet. At least part of the obstacle to his mum returning home had been removed, and that would have to do for the moment.

"Now," his dad said, "Tell me what really happened once more so I can make a little more sense of it all."

Daniel began his story again. As yet his dad's only explanation for what really happened in the tunnels was that Daniel had had an hallucination. He felt that Daniel hadn't really seen what he thought he'd seen. But Daniel knew differently. What he'd seen had been real enough but would he ever be able to explain it?

****

Next day Kelly's grandad called round in response to a phone call from Daniel's dad. He was invited in and he settled himself into an armchair

"Well I never thought I'd be grateful to a Palmer."

That comment was a red rag to Daniel's dad, "And what do you mean by that, may I ask? Just tell us exactly what you've got against our family."

"Surely I don't need to go over it again, but if you want it spelt out to you I will. Your father was a traitor and that's something I'll never forget."

"So is that what you've come round for this afternoon, to open old wounds? Isn't it about time you forgot all this nonsense. The war finished over thirty years ago you know. I thought you might have wanted to thank Daniel for saving your granddaughter's life."

"Well I think it was a pretty daft idea to keep a huge snake in your loft in the first place."

Daniel could see his dad getting really worked up. "And I suppose it was a clever idea of your granddaughter's to go and let her out of the loft. Is that what you think?"

"Now just you listen to me," Daniel's dad continued, "I'm going to say this now and I hope you'll get it into that thick Horton skull of yours...."

"I'm not listening to this," said Kelly's grandad. He made to get up from his chair but Daniel's dad put a hand on his shoulder.'

"Just sit down, you're not going anywhere until I've had my say. It strikes me that you've said far too much for far too long, and most of it is hogwash."

"You can't speak to me like that."

"Why not?" Daniel's dad was getting into his stride. "You've spoken like that to people for years now, it'll do you good to get a bit of your own medicine."

Kelly's grandad looked furious but he stayed where he was.

"I'll tell you what my dad was, he was an incredibly brave man."

There was a spluttering sound but Daniel's dad continued.

"I repeat, he was a very brave man. On the first count he was brave because he stood up for what he believed. He wouldn't be led blindly into doing something he felt wasn't right and so he spoke out against the war, against fighting."

On the second count, he was a compassionate man. He cared about others and it didn't matter what their nationality was. They were all human beings. That German pilot had surrendered and under the terms of the Geneva Convention he was entitled to fair treatment according to the rules of war.'

"Humbug," Kelly's grandad spat out the word. "At that time, the only good Jerry was a dead one. I was fighting them, I ought to know."

"And I suppose you'd have wanted all our pilots shot down over Germany to be treated like that too, would you, because that's what would have happened if you'd have taken the law into your own hands."

Kelly's grandad looked uncomfortable. He was about to reply when Daniel's dad butted in once more.

"And on the third count, I'll tell you something more about my dad, something you wouldn't have seen because you'd left the country again...."

"Yes, I was fighting, fighting for my country, not like some...."

"Just drop your prejudices a minute will you and listen. My dad was no coward. He may have been a little misguided in what he said and did and the way he got people's backs up with his pacifist talk, but he made up for it all right. After he'd helped that Jerry, he wouldn't take shelter ever again. He was up top in the fiercest of raids, out with the medical teams, pulling people from the wreckage of their houses. He was stubborn too, no one could persuade him to get down the tunnels. He may only have had his one arm but he worked as hard as anyone else. There are many people still alive in this town today who owe their lives to my dad.

"After the war there was a fierce argument over whether or not he should be recommended for a medal. He settled it himself, said he didn't want a medal. What he'd done was enough. So don't let me hear you say that he was a coward. He believed that killing people was wrong, whatever the reason, and he stood by his beliefs."

Daniel's dad sat down, exhausted by his outburst. Kelly's grandad said nothing. The room was quiet for several minutes.

"Are you going to have some tea with me?" Daniel's dad was on his feet again, then without waiting for an answer he walked through to the kitchen and filled the kettle. He called to Daniel to go and help him. Shortly afterwards, while Daniel was pouring milk into three cups, they both heard the front door open and close.

"He's left," Daniel said.

"I thought he would. It's tough facing up to the truth after all this time."

Daniel pictured Kelly's look of gratitude in the tunnels and thought how hard it was facing up to the truth at any time. He would have to tell her what really happened, he couldn't go on living with the lie.

Chapter Sixteen

After lunch, Daniel's dad said that he ought to call in at the zoo and just check that the snake was all right. He hoped that it hadn't suffered too much stress from its trip to the tunnels. It would probably be sleeping, he thought, but he felt that he at least owed the creature a visit.

Daniel was still somewhat confused by his dad's reaction the previous night. He had expected anger, punishment even, but instead the reverse had happened. His dad had talked a lot about how things would get better and he'd asked Daniel to give him another chance. Now Daniel needed to talk to someone himself and the only person who could possibly understand was his grandad.

Daniel left the house and looked warily around for any signs of the Horton gang. He didn't think there'd be any problems but he wasn't prepared to take chances. Halfway to his grandad's house he saw them and scooted down an alleyway. Then just as he was congratulating himself on his skill in escaping them, they reappeared, directly in front of him and he heard Selena's boom of a voice:

"Hey Daniel, Kelly wants to be your girlfriend. She......."

Whatever she would have said next was cut short by Kelly who put her arm round Selena's neck and her hand on her mouth. Louise and Dolly danced off at this point and started calling too.

"It's true, it's true, she loves you."

Kelly, it seemed was still having trouble controlling her gang, but Daniel wasn't prepared to wait around for the outcome of this fresh rebellion. He ran as fast as he could.

The very thought of having a girlfriend was bad enough, but to be linked romantically with Kelly Horton was a terrible prospect. He'd never hear the last of it from Errol.

Panting, he ran up the steps to his grandad's door and rang the bell for a long time.

"All right, all right, what's the fuss, where's the fire?" His grandad was coming, pulling back a bolt, turning a key.

As the door finally opened Daniel glanced round to see if he had been followed and then pushed past his grandad into the hallway.

"Don't mind me."

"Sorry grandad, it's just that those girls are after me again."

"You know Daniel, I'd give anything to go back to those days. Personally I don't see the problem. The time to worry is when they don't come after you. Anyway, come into the kitchen and I'll get us something to drink."

Daniel sat down with a lemonade. He didn't have to explain everything to his grandad because he'd seen an item all about the incident on the local news. He'd also had a talk with Daniel's dad on the telephone.

"So," his grandad said, "I'm sure that you haven't come round here using up a precious day of your half-term, just to talk about the weather. What's bothering you?"

Daniel's grandad listened attentively as Daniel briefly told his side of the story. When he reached the part where Kelly hit her head and the strange figure appeared, his grandad looked away and seemed to be staring into the distance. Then he coughed, and turned back to Daniel.

"I'll tell you one thing for certain, that wasn't the ghost of any German pilot."

"How do you know that Grandad?"

"Just tell me what he was saying again."

"It was something like - I've got you now, you'll be all

right."

"Well it's almost forty years since I first heard that voice, and up until now, I don't think I ever believed in ghosts. I guess I'm going to have to think again on that subject from now on."

"Yes, but who was it?"

"Well, my theory is that you met up with young Jimmy Dixon."

Daniel looked puzzled.

"Think back to the time that I told you about the crashed German pilot. Jimmy Dixon was the lad who helped me drag him to the tunnel steps. The lad who wasn't quite right in the head. And Daniel, I'll tell you what convinces me as to the truth of what you saw, he was saying those very same words when he was helping me."

"But why? What is he doing down there? What happened?"

"Hold on," his grandad said, "just wait a moment and I'll tell you."

He cleared his throat. "Jimmy Dixon was crazy, we all knew that, but I've never met a braver lad. He seemed to have no fear of fire or bombs. He'd be out every night in the midst of it all helping where he could and he didn't seem to understand that he could get hurt. For a while he seemed to have a charmed life, and anyone who stayed close by him seemed to be protected too. We all wanted to be with Jimmy in the thick of the action, he was our lucky mascot."

Daniel's grandad paused for a moment and stared away as if looking back across the decades.

"Then one night, not long after he'd saved that German's life, he copped it. We used to say that if a bomb had your name on it, you'd get it. This one must have had Jimmy's name written on it in mile high letters. It was a direct hit on one of the tunnel entrances. Jimmy had been sitting there all on his own, taking a break, probably eating a sandwich that his mum had made for him. Well there wasn't much left of Jimmy when they came to pick up the pieces."

Daniel saw that his grandad was reliving that moment. His face was screwed up and he tried to speak again but the words wouldn't come. It was quiet for a while but eventually he started again.

"I've never forgotten Jimmy. Some folks laughed at him and joked that he wasn't really much use. He'd just latch on to whoever was on duty and follow them round. But he'd do whatever you told him to."

Again a period of quiet.

"He was with me that night Daniel. I left him at the top of the steps while I delivered a message to the tunnels. And that's when the bomb got him. It blocked the tunnel entrance too. I had to run to the next entrance, get up top, and run back to where I'd left him, but I knew what I'd discover. He was way beyond my help. That was Jimmy Dixon who you saw Daniel, saving someone's life again...."

Daniel shivered. The room seemed to have suddenly turned very cold. "So you think I saw a ghost grandad. People always say they don't exist."

"Yes, I think you saw a ghost, Daniel. The ghost of Jimmy Dixon."

"And no one else will believe me, will they?"

"I don't think so Daniel."

" You know I'm really frightened to think that I actually saw him, but I'm really glad he was there."

****

On the first day back after the half-term holiday Mrs.

Francis was taking assembly with the whole of Barhampton Primary School. The hymn singing hadn't been very good, but that was nothing unusual Then it was time for a couple of notices before Mrs. Francis stepped forward again, and asked the school to sit down.

"I have something very important to say," she announced in a serious voice, "and I want you all to pay attention."

Everyone stopped fidgeting and looked towards their headteacher.

"Last half-term many children started to believe that there is a ghost in our school, the ghost of a German airman who crashed his plane on our school grounds during the last war. This led to some very silly behaviour."

There was a buzz of conversation which was quickly hushed by teachers at the sides of the hall.

"I now have evidence," Mrs. Francis continued, "to show that there couldn't possibly be a ghost. The German pilot did not die in the plane crash, nor did he die from his injuries. He spent some time in a British hospital before being taken to a prisoner of war camp. After the war he returned to Germany."

Again a buzz of conversation.

"What is more," Mrs. Francis raised her voice, "I have a letter in German, sent to me from Germany. Does anyone here speak German?"

Everyone looked round but no one raised a hand.

"Actually, I know that Mr. Metcalfe speaks German quite well. Would you come and translate for us please?"

Mr. Metcalfe looked a little worried as he made his way to the front of the hall. He took the letter and was surprised to find that it was already partly translated.

Mrs. Francis smiled, "When you're ready."

Dear Children,

As you can see I am very much alive. I am sorry if this has spoilt your fun. It is always good to have a mystery to solve. But as you see, there is no mystery about me and I am not haunting your school.

My very best wishes to you all,
Herman Grunweld.

It was impossible to quell the noise that started up when Mr. Metcalfe had finished reading. Mrs. Francis didn't even try. She waited patiently until it subsided and then began again.

"So you see, children, the ghost does not exist, and I think that puts paid to all the rumours that have been flying around. Please tell your parents that there is nothing to worry about and that our school is a ghost-free zone!"

She turned and left the hall. Mr. Metcalfe followed her outside.

"Clever," he said, "I like it. But tell me one thing, why did you have your fingers crossed when I read out the letter?"

"I have to confess, Mike, that I didn't tell the whole truth."

"What do you mean?"

"That letter was actually from a friend of mine in Munich. Herman Grunweld existed all right but he couldn't be traced. We just decided to compose the sort of letter he might well have written if it had been possible to contact him."

"You mean it was a lie?"

"I wouldn't call it lying, Mike. It's just that sometimes headteachers, like politicians and Presidents of the United States, are allowed to be a little economical with the truth!"

Mr. Metcalfe laughed, "It'll catch up with you."

"Maybe, if I'm unlucky. But till then, I think I've solved our problem."

****

On the way home from school that evening, Daniel was with Errol. Something seemed to have sapped Errol's energy as he seemed quite content to drift along at a slow pace. This certainly suited Daniel as he wanted to ask his friend's advice. He'd already tried to explain to Errol what had happened in the tunnels but he knew that his friend found it hard to believe.

"What would you do in my place?" Daniel asked.

"About what?"

"About Kelly. Should I tell her what really happened?"

"No. Absolutely not. One reason being that she'll never believe you. She'll think that you've gone crazy. Not only that she'll broadcast it to everyone and they'll all think you're crazy too."

"Is there another reason?"

"Yes. Just let her carry on thinking that you saved her life. We certainly don't owe her any favours and if we don't have to skulk around in fear of the Horton gang for a while, then that's all to the good. So do us all a favour Daniel and go along with what she thinks. Besides, I can't see any way that she's ever going to discover anything else."

"What do you mean?"

"Well," Errol continued, "If what you say really happened...."

"It did happen Errol, there's no 'if' about it."

"OK, OK, so Kelly's hardly likely to find out the truth is she? This Jimmy Dixon, he's hardly likely to be popping up to say hello, is he?"

"Yes, I know that you're right Errol, but I'm still not happy about it."

"Well, I'm happy about it, we'll all be happy about it, if it means that we don't get to test out the suction power of the Horton gang's lips."

Daniel smiled. He certainly felt better now. With the disappearance of the snake it seemed as if a great weight had been lifted. He'd certainly slept well for the past few nights knowing that the snake wasn't over his head. And another thing too, his mum was coming round for tea tonight. His dad had even taken the afternoon off work to go and buy some food.

Daniel was feeling good. He broke into a run and called over his shoulder to Errol, "I bet I can beat you home tonight."